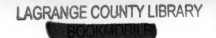

Fayette

A Time to Love

Donna Winters

Great Lakes Romances®

Bigwater Publishing
Caledonia, Michigan

Acknowledgements

I would like to thank Brenda Laakso, Site Historian, Fayette Historic Townsite, for generously providing research materials and guidance throughout the development, writing, and pre-publication phases of this book.

I would also like to thank my cherished friend, Joanne Olson, for reading the story before it went to press.

Note

Although the young of a fox are commonly called "kits", in this story, I have used the old-fashioned expression, "cubs".

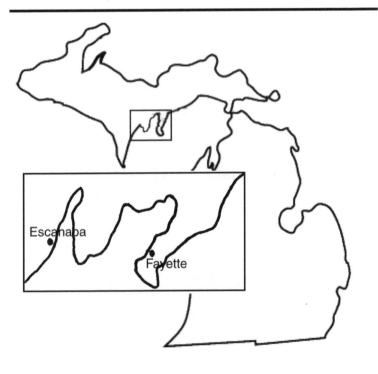

Chapter

1

Fayette, Michigan
April 1, 1868

"You disgrace to ol' Eire!"

"You son of a sea cook!"

Workers had just emerged from the iron-smelting furnace at the end of the first shift and already two of them were shouting epithets at each other.

"A fine way to spoil a balmy spring day," muttered sixteen-year-old Lavinia McAdams.

Clutching her parcel to her bosom, she paused on the step of the company store long enough to see Big Billy Bassett, a renowned pugilist in the village, knock the cap off a shorter, stockier fellow, revealing the unmistakable red, wavy hair of an Irishman.

Fists flew.

Furnace workers gathered around, egging on the pair. The Irishman's muscle-bound arms landed punches that disappeared within the bulk of Big Billy Bassett's stomach. Where were her father and the other furnace supervisors? Knowing the quarrelsome natures of their men, they should have been on hand to break up the fight.

Disgusted with the contentiousness of the laborers, Lavinia turned to go, bumping headlong into an auburn-haired young woman and knocking her basket clear from her hand. Eggs flew out and smashed to the ground.

The girl's wide-set blue eyes flashed with anger. "Now there's a fine kettle of fish you've put me in! And how am I to pay for my washboard, pray tell?"

"I'm so sorry!" Lavinia exclaimed, picking up the basket and returning it to the owner whose lovely face was marred only by her scowl. "It was all my fault. We'll put your washboard on my father's account."

"And who might your father be?" she asked skeptically.

"Angus McAdams."

Much mellowed, the young woman smiled. "Angus McAdams! Well, now. My brother-in-law, Paddy O'Connell, works for him!"

Returning to the store, Lavinia made things right for the girl who introduced herself as Moira Cleary. She appeared to be a couple of years older than Lavinia, and said she was working as a laundress while living with her sister's family in one of the log cabin shanties near the shore. Despite the girl's decidedly comely appearance, Lavinia couldn't help noticing that beneath her woolen shawl, she wore a frayed white apron and a calico dress with many patches.

Parting from Moira amicably, Lavinia hurried along the crushed limestone street toward the red-sided, white trimmed homes that the Jackson Iron Company had built for its supervisors—one small island of civilization in this wild, untamed wilderness. Images of the fistfight coming to mind, her thoughts entered into a conflict of their own. How she had learned to loathe this raw, unrefined village in the six months she had been living here! Neither schoolhouse nor church adorned its landscape, forcing her folks to hold family tutoring sessions and worship services at their dining table.

But that wasn't the worst part of living at Fayette. Its stinking, soot-spewing furnace and shrieking steam whistles tainted the fresh breezes off the bay and drowned out the songs of sparrows, robins, and cardinals in the surrounding hardwoods. She didn't care much for the town's dirt-smudged, uneducated immigrants, either. The laundress and the Irishman pugilist probably couldn't read or write. And that fellow should have known better than to let Big Billy Bassett entice him into a battle. You didn't have to live in Fayette more than a day or two to learn that!

Thank goodness, in another four months and seven days, she would turn seventeen, and would have her folks' permission to return to her hometown in Canada.

But she couldn't think about that now. She must get home and set the biscuits to baking for the chicken stew she and her mother had prepared at her father's request. When he came home for the midday meal, he said he had invited a supper guest, but had refused to say whom. And he had instructed her to go to the company store late in the afternoon, pick up a package that would be waiting for her, and carry it, unopened, to her mother.

"No peeking, or it will turn into a pumpkin. You'll see!" he had teased.

She wondered what lay hidden inside the brown paper tied with string. It was too soft to be the school slates her mother frequently wished for in hopes of tutoring the poor, uneducated immigrant children living in the crude log cabins by the shore. From the feel of it, it could be a new tablecloth, or the lace curtains that her mother had so badly wanted for the front window. That must be it! Lace curtains! And the guest would be none other than Mr. Harris, the company superintendent! She hurried faster.

Twenty minutes later, while her biscuits baked, Lavinia

stood before the dresser mirror in the cramped attic bed-room she shared with her six-year-old sister, Flora, admiring her new blue cotton dress—her very first long dress! The package was special indeed, a brand new spring dress handmade by her Grandma Ferguson to replace the out-grown one she had worn all winter long. Grandma had also sent a plain white shirt for Lavinia's eleven-year-old brother, Toby, and a pink dress for Flora. Her father's warning to carry the package home unopened had been a ruse to ensure that the gifts remained a secret until everyone gathered together to share the joy of discovering their grandmother's surprise.

How Lavinia wished her mirror was full-length so she could see the three rows of flounces at the bottom of the skirt, and the way they gently brushed the floor when she moved. For now, she would have to settle for a view of the bodice. She read again the note her grandmother enclosed with the garment.

> *Dearest Lavinia,*
> *Wear this dress in good health, with a smile on your face, and fond memories of your dear old grandma.*
> *How I miss you and your mama and papa and sister and brother! I look forward to the day I will see you all again. Until then, my love and prayers are with you.*
> *Affectionately,*
> *Grandma*

Tomorrow, she would write to Grandma to thank her for the wonderful gifts, telling how she had been certain they were curtains for Mama's bare parlor window until she had opened the parcel and discovered the most wonderful surprise since moving to Fayette.

From downstairs, the anticipation in her mother's voice floated up to her. "Lavinia, how does it look? I'm eager to see!"

"I'll be down in a minute, Mama!"

She picked up the fancy print scarf that had come with the dress, drew it around her neck, and fastened it with the pewter pin her grandmother had given to her last fall before the move to Fayette from Canada.

Flora, in her new pink dress, stood beside the bureau clutching Tilly, the rag doll she had worn out with love, and watching Lavinia's every move. "You're so pretty, Livvy! I hope when I grow up I'll be as pretty as you!"

Lavinia tossed back her dark, shoulder-length hair, bent down, and gazed into her sister's freckled face. "You'll be even prettier, Flora! You look especially fine in your new dress. Now let's go downstairs."

Flora skipped out of the room, her sandy-colored braids bouncing behind. Before Lavinia reached the stairs, she heard her father coming through the door and Toby announcing him with an enthusiastic, "Papa's home!"

Angus McAdams' booming voice carried up the stairs. "I smell my favorite chicken stew and biscuits!"

By the time Lavinia reached the bottom step, her brother, sister, and mother, eager for their customary hugs, had already surrounded him. Lavinia paused. A moment later, he gazed up at her, his entire face lighting up.

"Lavinia! How lovely you look—and so grown up." Leaving the others, he took her by the hand, escorting her off the last step. His blue eyes glistened and his voice grew sentimental. "Seems like only yesterday you were but a wee lass, and now look at you! Your pretty smile and dark hair are the image of your mother at your age, too beautiful for words!"

Lavinia hugged his neck and kissed his cheek. "Thank you, Papa!"

Her mother drew near, smiling approvingly. "You look lovely, indeed, Lavinia. Now, I could use your help in the kitchen. Your biscuits are about ready to come out of the oven. Our guest will be here at any minute."

"I'll be right there, Mama!" To her father, she said, "I had a little accident on my way out of the store." She explained about Moira Cleary's eggs and the washboard charged to his account, adding a heartfelt apology for the extra expense she'd caused.

He kissed her forehead. "Never mind. Some accidents can't be avoided. Now, go and help your mother."

She started for the kitchen, then turned back. "You never told us who is coming to dinner."

"So I didn't. The gentleman's name is Mr. Harri—"

"Mr. Harris!" Lavinia exclaimed. Her father started to say something, but Lavinia rushed on in her excitement. "I just knew the superintendent would be coming! Oh, Papa, you'll be proud of the dinner we'll serve him tonight. Mama's chicken stew is the best she's ever made, and my biscuits will be light as air, I promise!"

The last she heard as she darted for the kitchen was Flora's childish voice declaring, "I helped make the mince-meat pie, Papa!"

Lavinia and Flora set the table with their mother's good china—Lavinia's favorite because of the romantic vignettes painted in blue against a white porcelain background. Lavinia tasted the stew one last time as a knock sounded at the front door. Angus's voice boomed from the master bedroom where he was changing to a clean shirt. "Lavinia, will you please invite our guest in?"

"Of course, Papa!"

10

She made haste up the hall to the front door. Opening it wide, she gasped at the sight of the fellow standing there, then slammed it shut and all but ran back down the hall, colliding with her father and brother.

"Papa, there's a perfectly awful red-haired Irishman outside the door!"

Toby ran to the front window. "He's got red hair, all right, and a nifty-looking cap in his hand!"

"Son, come away from the window," Angus said, then turned to Lavinia. "Why didn't you invite him in?"

"I . . . Mr. Harris will be arriving at any moment!"

Her father grinned. "Who ever said Mr. Harris was coming to dinner?"

"You did!"

He shook his head. "I tried to tell you that Mr. *Harrigan* would be coming, but you didn't let me finish. Now go and invite Mr. Harrigan in."

"But Papa, you don't understand! This Harrigan fellow is nothing but a—a *hoodlum!* I saw him in a fistfight outside the furnace just after work today. Surely you don't mean to sit down to dinner with the likes of *him!*"

"I most assuredly do! And so shall you. Now go and see him in."

Lavinia returned to the door. Drawing a deep breath, she opened it—and her mouth—but before she could get a word out, the Harrigan fellow, with a wide grin and a bob of his head, spoke up, his words free of the usual brogue.

"Good evening, Miss McAdams! I'm Huck Harrigan. Quite an April Fool's joke you played, slamming the door in my face. For a minute, I really wondered if you were going to let me in! But Mr. McAdams wouldn't have invited me over here just to keep me standing at the door, I'm certain." He paused, but when she remained silent, he asked

11

boldly, "You don't mind if I come in now, do you?" He stepped past her into the entryway.

Overwhelmed by the flow of words coming at her, and the flood of thoughts through her head, she couldn't seem to make her tongue work. Instead, she simply gaped.

He hung his tweed cap and jacket on the tree stand and stood smiling at her. Smiling and silent.

Lavinia offered a smile that turned into laughter and gave way to an explanation. "The joke was on me, Mr. Harrigan. I was expecting someone entirely different. Now come into the parlor. Papa's waiting for you."

Following handshakes all around, Mary McAdams, the proper hostess, announced, "Dinner's ready. If you'll all be seated, Lavinia and I will bring out the stew and biscuits."

Flora said, "Let me help, too, Mama!"

"You may show Mr. Harrigan to his place at the table," Mary told her.

Without a moment's hesitation, Flora took Huck by the hand, saying, "You're sitting in Toby's place, across from Livvy tonight, and he's sitting at the end, next to Mama."

When plates were filled and Lavinia had taken her seat, her father said, "Mr. Harrigan, since you're our guest this evening, would you please ask the blessing?"

"I'd be honored." He bowed his head. "May the furnace burn hot and the iron flow. May the sun shine warm and a gentle breeze blow. May the stew and the biscuits be tasty today, and blessings greet us all along our way. Amen."

Seemingly at will, Huck had lapsed into an Irish brogue. The lilt of his baritone voice and his delightful words lifted Lavinia's spirit, making her first taste of stew and biscuits more delectable than expected.

Huck paused after his first bite, his gaze taking in both

her and her mother. "Mrs. McAdams, Miss McAdams, your stew and biscuits are more than tasty, they're *excellent!*"

Mary beamed. "Thank you, Mr. Harrigan! My daughter is truly the biscuit expert in this family."

Lavinia smiled, a warmth invading her cheeks. She didn't know why the compliment should cause her such discomfort; she only knew that she must change the subject. Looking Huck directly in the eye, she asked, "That was you I saw in a fistfight with Big Billy Bassett after work today, wasn't it?"

Huck nodded, swallowing a mouthful of stew to make a reply, but Lavinia went on before he could explain.

"See, Papa? I told you he was a hoodlum, and he admits it!"

Toby rushed to Huck's defense. "He can't be a hoodlum! No hoodlum wears a cap as neat as Mr. Harrigan's!"

Angus flashed his son a warning look. "Toby, you know the rule, no arguing at the table."

"Sorry, Papa." He quickly turned to Huck. "Can I try on your cap after supper?"

Huck smiled. "You may." Focusing on Lavinia, he met her disapproving gaze. "As for the fistfight, there's a perfectly logical explanation. It wasn't a fight, it was more like . . . an exhibition."

"An exhibition?" she asked incredulously. "Is that what you call it when two fellows are taking swings at each other, looking for all the world like they intend to knock each other flat?"

Toby spoke up. "Lavinia's arguing, Papa! She should be sent to her room!"

"Hush, son. Let Mr. Harrigan have his say."

Huck explained. "Actually, Billy and I called our tussle

13

an April Fool's joke, better known on any other day of the year as a convincing job of pulling punches!"

Lavinia remained adamant. "But I saw you bury your fist in Billy's stomach—twice!"

Flora's eyes grew wide. "Did you really, Mr. Harrigan? Did you really hit Big Billy Bassett in the tummy?"

Huck shook his head. "It was all pretend, Flora. We were just putting on a show."

Lavinia remained skeptical. "For what purpose?"

His gaze met hers. "It's a hot, hard, and dirty job we do, day in and day out. We just couldn't resist a little prank!" His eyes twinkled as he explained how he and Billy had practiced their moves and made their plans in secret, then went to work pretending to be angry and ready to fight after their shift. Paddy O'Connell, who was known to make wagers on everything from the weather to the number of iron pigs the furnace would produce on a given day, set odds and took bets.

Angus said, "Huck and Billy had asked me about the prank and I told them to go ahead. I thought Paddy knew, too."

"The wagers were all part of the joke," Huck explained. "After Billy and I went at it for a while, he took a fall. All the fellows were hovering over him, wondering how I could have hit hard enough to knock the big fellow out, when all of a sudden he jumped up and shouted 'April Fool!' Paddy sparked and sputtered when he found out he had to return the money, but a well-aimed bucket of water cooled his temper."

Mary smiled. "All's well that ends well, then."

"That's not quite the end of it," Huck informed her with a smile. "Your husband has often spoken of how you wished for school slates to instruct the immigrant children in the three R's. Just before Paddy gave the money back, I did manage to talk a few of the fellows into giving up their wagers for that good purpose." Pulling a knotted handkerchief from his pocket, he set it on the table with a clink. "It's not much, but it's enough to make a start."

Mary swiftly unknotted the handkerchief and counted the coins. "Bless your heart, Mr. Harrigan, and *thank you!* You are truly amazing!"

Lavinia silently disagreed. She couldn't help wondering what other tricks Huck Harrigan had up his sleeve. So far, he had passed off a fistfight as a charitable deed, and convinced her parents that he was not a hoodlum, but an honorable fellow. Was there nothing he couldn't whitewash with his glib tongue and ready smile? She was pondering the question when Huck's words, in answer to a query from her mother, captured her attention.

"My mother and dad came over from the north of Ireland in '47 and settled on a piece of farmland west of Milwaukee. My sister was born in '48, I came along in '50, then my brother and two more sisters after that."

Now Lavinia understood why Huck seemed so thoroughly Irish, able to speak with or without a brogue. She listened with interest as he continued.

"For years, there wasn't any school we could attend, and Mama was too busy raising my younger brother and sisters and helping Dad on the farm to teach us to read. Then one day, a nice lady came to visit. Her husband had taken up farming down the road. They had a son and a daughter about the same age as Kathleen and me. Mrs. Ryan said if my sister and I would come over to her place each day when we'd finished our morning chores, she'd teach us to read and write along with her own kids. I've always wished I could repay Mrs. Ryan for her kindness, but she's been long gone. It seems only fitting and proper that I help you to pass on the gift of reading to the young ones here at Fayette."

Aglow with enthusiasm, Mary exclaimed, "I'll order slates tomorrow!"

Angus said, "In the meantime, we'll need to find some scholars. I'll ask around at work. I ought to be able to find some fellows who will want to send their young ones here for tutoring sessions until we can build a schoolhouse."

Toby spoke up. "You mean we're going to have those dirty shanty kids sitting at this table?"

Flora at the same moment declared, "I can hardly wait! I want to make some new friends!"

Lavinia wished she shared her sister's innocent enthusiasm. She'd seen muddy, ragamuffin kids playing outside the log cabins. The thought of them sitting here at this very table with her mother and Toby and Flora for reading lessons made her shudder.

Angus leveled his gaze on Toby. "The kids over in the shanties deserve the same opportunity for schooling as you do, son."

"I won't sit next to them!"

"Toby, go to your room," Angus said firmly. "I warned you about arguing at the table."

"Don't I even get a piece of mincemeat pie?"

"No. Now go." Angus pointed to the door.

Toby set down his fork with a clank and shuffled out of the room.

Angus told Huck, "I'm sorry about Toby's rudeness. He will apologize to you himself before you leave tonight."

Huck said, "I'm sorry for *him*. He doesn't seem to realize that if this town had a school, he'd be sitting next to the lads from the shanties, like it or not."

Mary said, "Will you please point that out to him when he comes down to apologize? I can tell already that he really likes you."

"At least he likes my cap!" Huck allowed. "I'll be glad to talk with him if you think it will help."

The conversation turned to Huck's family, and he told of his aunts, uncles, and cousins, as well as his three sisters and brother in Wisconsin. Lavinia feigned disinterest. Huck tried to elicit some response from her, sharing a couple of humorous Irish limericks his uncles had taught him, but she remained silent as a stone.

Then Flora served everyone pieces of her mincemeat pie, presenting him with an especially wide slice. She watched intently as Huck took a bite of the pastry. Swallowing a mouthful of sweet filling and flaky crust, he said, "Miss Flora, your pie could win a ribbon at the county fair!"

The little girl grinned from braid to braid. "Do you really think so, Mr. Harrigan?"

"Without a doubt!"

Dessert was soon over, and Mary asked everyone to adjourn to the parlor where she returned to the subject of Huck's family. "You haven't said much about your folks. Are they still on the farm?"

Huck shook his head, saying only that they had died in an accident when he was ten. "What I remember most about my kin in Wisconsin is the fun we'd have when we played our penny whistles. I took the liberty of bringing mine along—it's in my jacket pocket. I'll play for you if you'd like."

Angus nodded. "By all means."

Huck retrieved his whistle. Lavinia saw him pause in the hallway a moment followed by the shrug of his shoulders before he entered the parlor. Without a word, he began playing *Gary Owen,* a spirited folk tune from old Ireland. Flora was so taken by the quick rhythm that she got up and began to dance with her doll, Tilly. Huck gave her an impromptu lesson in the heel-toe steps of a simple jig, then continued piping, heartened by her enthusiasm—so contagious that both Angus and Mary joined her with some fancy footwork of their own. After a few rounds of *The Galway Piper,* an equally lively number, he played *Tarry Trousers,* a love song of a more moderate tempo. Then he sang a verse, his gaze often on Lavinia.

> *Yonder stands a pretty maiden,*
> *Who she is I do not know,*
> *I'll go court her for her beauty,*
> *Let her answer yes or no.*

> *'Pretty maid, I've come to court you,*
> *If your favour I do gain*
> *And you make me hearty welcome,*
> *I will call this way again.'*

Lavinia remained silent, her expression unreadable. The infuriating fellow hardly seemed to notice. Ignoring her withdrawn attitude, he continued to play and sing, encouraged by the hearty applause of her parents and sister. Time slipped away. The light of day dimmed and Mary lit the oil lamps.

"I'd better go," Huck said.

Angus said, "I'll fetch Toby, and he will apologize."

When he had gone upstairs, Mary said, "Mr. Harrigan, please remember to tell Toby what you said earlier about the shanty kids and school."

"I'll remember," Huck promised.

Mary took Flora by the hand. "Say goodnight to Mr. Harrigan, then we'll go upstairs. It's way past your bedtime."

"Good night Mr. Harrigan! Promise you'll come again, *please!*"

"If you invite me, I'll come!" Huck agreed.

"Oh, *good!*" Flora replied, chattering excitedly to Tilly and her mother about his next visit as they left the room.

Alone with Huck, Lavinia found the parlor far too quiet. An eternity seemed to pass before Angus and Toby entered the room.

The young boy approached, head down, Huck's cap in hand. "I'm sorry for arguing. And I'm sorry I took your cap." He offered it to Huck, and promptly turned to go.

"Not so fast, young man! I've got a couple of things to say to you. Come sit down." Huck indicated the chair near his.

Toby did as Huck said, chin low. Angus sat, too.

"First of all, Toby, I accept your apologies. It takes real character to own up to your mistakes."

Toby gazed silently at his shoes.

Huck continued. "As for the shanty kids coming here to learn, when I was your age, I'd have felt the same way you do."

Toby looked up, a question in his eyes.

Huck repeated, "I'd have felt the same way, and I'd have been wrong. You see, Toby, not too long from now, this town will put up a school where all the children can go to learn. Then, you'll have no say over who sits beside you."

Instantly angry, Toby insisted, "I'll sit by myself! I wish we'd never left Canada!" He darted from the room.

"Toby! Wait!"

The youngster paid no heed to Huck's call, heading out the front door into the dark of night.

Huck ran after him, Angus close behind.

Lavinia rose from her silent perch on the sofa. Leaving the problem of Toby to Huck and her father, she headed for the kitchen. As she cleaned up the dishes, she pondered Toby's words, longing as he did for the happy days of Canada. She didn't blame Toby one bit for running out on that Harrigan fellow. Who did he think he was, anyway, trying to convince her little brother that he should like those shanty kids?

Her mother came downstairs from tucking in Flora. "Has Mr. Harrigan taken his leave already? I meant to say goodnight to him. And where are your father and brother?"

Lavinia had no sooner explained than the three fellows came through the front door. Her mother joined them in the entryway, returning to the kitchen with her father moments later.

He handed Lavinia a towel. "Dry your hands and see Mr. Harrigan out, please. He's waiting to bid you good-night."

Reluctantly, she did as her father asked.

Huck was waiting just inside the front door. "Thank you kindly for your hospitality, Miss McAdams. I pray we'll meet again soon." He pulled his cap over his thick red hair and stepped out the front door.

"Mr. Harrigan?"

He turned to her, a look of expectation clearly visible, even in the dim light spilling from the open door.

She continued. "My father likes you well enough to invite you to supper. My mother likes your charitable nature. Toby loves your cap, and Flora thinks you're a gift from heaven. But as far as *I'm* concerned, you're still nothing but a hoodlum!"

She shut the door with a thud.

Putting his whistle to his lips, Huck piped his way to the hotel, pausing to rest a moment on the front steps. The parting words from Miss Lavinia McAdams had nearly put him off key. Her fetching figure, shiny brown hair, delightful blue dress, and lighthearted laughter had quickly captured his attention. Now, if he could only change her opinion of him . . .

Chapter

2

Thunder rumbled and rain poured down, running in streams off the umbrella Huck carried in one hand, the other clutching the bundle of slates and slate pencils that had just been unpacked late this afternoon at the company store. The manager, having seen Toby and Huck together in his establishment half a dozen times in the last three weeks, asked if he would pass word along that the goods had arrived the next time he saw a member of the McAdams family. Huck jumped at the chance to volunteer to deliver them right away, even though he was weary to the bone and eager for a big dinner and a quiet and restful Saturday night.

The furnace was shut down for the day tomorrow for repairs and adjustments to the blowing engine. After four long months of twelve-hour days, seven days a week, he would have plenty of time to rest before the 5 o'clock whistle called him back to work on Monday morning. He thought about Mary and Angus. The smiles brightening their faces when they opened the package would make his trip in the downpour worthwhile. Toby was sure to welcome him with enthusiasm and Flora with a little dance, but he braced himself for the cool reception Lavinia would offer. In brief encounters since their first meeting, he had learned that one disapproving glance from her frigid brown eyes could chill him more effectively than this cold spring rain.

He stepped up to the door and knocked. Toby opened it, his face brightening the gray day. "Huck! I sure wasn't expecting to see you out in this storm!"

Huck folded his umbrella and stepped onto the entryway rug, rain dripping from his shoes and trousers. "I've brought something for your folks."

Flora came running from the parlor to demand a hug and dance her jig. Her parents emerged from the kitchen, followed by Lavinia.

Angus and Mary greeted him in turn.

"What brings you all the way up here in such disagreeable weather?"

"Will you stay to dinner?"

To Huck's surprise, before he could answer, Lavinia had set his umbrella in the hall stand and was helping him off with his damp jacket, saying, "I'll hang this in the kitchen by the stove."

He wondered, as his gaze followed her feminine retreat down the hall, whether her frigid manner had begun to thaw, but he couldn't be certain. He offered his parcel to Mary. "These came in for you at the store. I thought you'd like to have them right away."

"The slates?"

Huck nodded.

Angus smiled. "Answered prayer."

Mary set the package on the hall table to unwrap it, inspecting the slates one at a time as if they were precious slabs of marble. "Think of all the learning that can be done on these," she said thoughtfully. Focusing on Huck, she said, "You *will* stay to dinner, won't you?"

Before he could answer, Toby said, "Please stay!"

And Flora added, "*Please*, Mr. Harrigan!"

Huck hesitated, unwilling to endure another meal

chilled by Lavinia's frosty glare.

Angus said, "Of course, if you have other plans for the evening, we understand."

In the kitchen, Lavinia apparently heard the invitation. She returned to the front hall, her gaze squarely on Huck. "We're having fish chowder tonight, and biscuits."

Though Lavinia hadn't quite smiled when she said it, Huck could see warmth in her brown eyes instead of the usual icy sheen. "I'd be a fool to pass on your biscuits, Miss McAdams!"

Lavinia returned to the kitchen with her mother to finish dinner preparations while the others settled in the parlor. As she worked her biscuit ingredients into small crumbs, she thought about the changes in her little brother since Huck had come into his life. On the night of their first meeting, when Toby had dashed out of the house angry, Huck had somehow managed to transform the runaway into an ally. She still wondered what Huck had said to turn her brother around. Three times, she had asked, only to be informed by her younger brother that it was none of her business.

After the rocky start to their friendship, Huck had twice weekly taken Toby fishing and then to the store for a candy stick, in the process changing his mind about tutoring the shanty kids. Additionally, the project had been a matter of daily prayer morning and night at family meals. As a result, several men at the furnace had agreed to send their children for lessons in reading, writing, and ciphering.

Huck's enthusiasm for the tutoring idea and the power of prayer had made Lavinia realize that her own opinions must change, both about the tutoring and about Huck. She couldn't argue against her parents' desire to help those less fortunate. And no longer could she see Huck as just a hoodlum.

She rolled out her dough, cut the biscuits, and was sliding the tray into the oven when she heard a commotion at the front door. Her father's voice carried down the hall all the way to the kitchen.

"Billy! Who have you got there? Come in out of the rain!"

She slammed the oven door with a clank, wiped her hands on her apron, and went to see who was there. She'd gone halfway down the hall, her mother at her heels, when she saw Big Billy Bassett coming through the door.

He was carrying a younger fellow on his shoulders, saying, "Don't know his name, but he's out cold."

Angus said, "Take him into the parlor and lay him on the sofa!"

Huck helped Billy to ease his burden onto the couch. "Where'd you come across this sack of potatoes, anyway, Billy?"

"He showed up at the hotel—collapsed on the front porch. I was the first to take notice. Was on my way up to Doc Sloane's with him."

Lavinia quickly divested the fair-haired stranger of his mud-caked boots, giving vent to the odor of wet woolen socks that had evidently avoided the washboard for weeks. As she carried the boots to the front hall, she heard her father tell Billy, "Go and fetch the good doctor. We'll see what we can do to bring the fellow around."

Billy wasted no time heading out the front door.

Back in the parlor, her mother sent Huck and Toby to fetch wash water and soap, and Flora to find some clean towels. Then she began to remove the stranger's jacket. "I wonder if he has anything in his pockets telling who he is or where he's from?" She searched the jacket while Angus

25

checked the stranger's trouser pockets, finding nothing more than a soggy, badly soiled handkerchief.

Lavinia noticed that the stranger appeared to be about her age. And his face, though smudged with dirt and pale nigh unto transparent, was nothing short of handsome. She was wondering what color eyes lay hidden beneath his closed lids when Huck, Toby, and Flora returned with the water, soap, and towels.

Immediately, Lavinia worked up some suds on the end of a towel and began to gently wash the grime from the stranger's face while her mother went to work on his dirt-caked hands. The others gathered close, watching the unconscious patient for any sign of response.

His eyelids twitched, then blinked several times before revealing the most engaging blue eyes Lavinia had ever seen. He stared at her a moment, then said, "I must have died and gone to heaven, and you must be one of my angels!"

Everyone laughed except Lavinia, whose cheeks grew hot. The sound of voices prompted a new observation from the patient, who began to look around the room. "Guess this ain't heaven after all, is it?"

Toby answered. "No, it's Fayette. What's your name?"

The fellow looked at him and smiled a most innocent smile. "What's *your* name?"

"Toby."

"That's my name, too! Toby!"

Lavinia didn't miss the looks of skepticism exchanged by her parents.

Huck asked the stranger, "Where are you from, Toby?"

His brow furrowed. "I . . . I don't remember."

Angus asked, "What *do* you remember?"

After a moment's thought, he shrugged. "Not much,

'cept bein' cold, wet, and hungry."

Mary said, "We can fix that, soon as the doctor has a look at you."

Flora stepped forward. "We're having fish chowder and biscuits for dinner, and Mama's best taffy tarts!"

Lavinia sprang to her feet. "I almost forgot my biscuits!" By the time she had removed them from their tray, Billy had returned with the doctor. She set her biscuits in the warming oven and hurried to the parlor.

After listening to Toby's heart, Dr. Sloane checked for evidence of head injuries, but found none. Then he began asking questions.

"What's your last name, Toby?"

He shrugged.

"Where do you live?"

"I don't remember."

"How old are you?"

"Fifteen."

He was a year younger than Lavinia had thought, if indeed he had remembered correctly. Still, he looked every bit as grown up as a sixteen-year-old.

Dr. Sloane asked, "Do you have any brothers or sisters?"

"No."

"What are your parents' names?"

"I don't know."

"Have you got any relatives in these parts?"

He shook his head.

With a kind smile, Dr. Sloane asked, "Is there any chance that some good victuals and rest will improve your memory?"

Toby grinned. "I'm sure of it!"

"Then I prescribe a hot meal and a good night's sleep.

Maybe tomorrow you'll remember where home is."

"Maybe tomorrow I'll remember where home is," Toby repeated parrot-like.

Mary said, "You may stay with us tonight, if you like."

Angus said, "I'll loan you a dry nightshirt, and you can sleep right here on the sofa."

Billy headed for the door. "I'll be on my way, then. You coming, Huck?"

He shook his head. "Not just yet. You go on without me."

Lavinia saw Billy out. The doctor and her parents joined her in the front hallway.

Her father told the doctor, "I'm much obliged to you, coming on a night such as this. I'll settle up with you on Monday. From what I can tell, the boy hasn't got a penny to his name."

Mary said, "Speaking of names, I'm not entirely convinced that the boy's real name is Toby."

Lavinia added, "And it seems odd that he hasn't even got so much as a goose egg yet most of his memory is missing."

Dr. Sloane tapped himself on the side of the head. "That isn't all he's missing up here. Unless he shows drastic improvement real soon, the best we can do is put a notice in some newspapers and hope his kin will come for him."

Angus said, "I'll see to it first of the week." He opened the door. "Good night, Doc. Again, thanks."

With a nod, Dr. Sloane stepped out into the rain that had diminished to a drizzle.

While the fellows helped the new Toby to change into a nightshirt and bed down on the sofa, Lavinia, Flora, and Mary finished dinner preparations, setting an extra place for Huck at the table and preparing a tray for the ailing Toby.

Lavinia carried the tray to the parlor, Flora close behind. "Dinner's ready," she announced to her brother, father, and Huck. "Mama says to come to the table."

Huck immediately took the tray from Lavinia. "I'll keep Toby company. Tell your mother to start without me."

Lavinia turned to Flora. "Tell Mama that Huck and I will be there shortly."

The others left, and Huck carried the tray to the sofa where the new Toby propped himself up to receive it. Ignoring the napkin and spoon, he lifted the bowl of broth to his lips and drank noisily. By the time Huck had put chairs for Lavinia and himself alongside the sofa, Toby had gobbled down the buttered biscuit as well. With a smack of his lips and a swipe of the napkin across his mouth, he smiled up at Lavinia. "They sure don't make biscuits like those back in Marquette!"

Huck said, "Is that where you're from, Toby? Marquette?"

The boy's smile vanished. He lowered his gaze. "Did I say Marquette? I didn't mean to." He suddenly looked up, fear evident in his blue eyes. "I don't know where I'm from! I just don't know!"

Lavinia glanced at Huck, reading the same doubt in his eyes that she was feeling inside.

Huck said, "That's okay, Toby. Maybe it will come to you."

Toby said, "Say, mister, are you her brother?" He pointed to Lavinia.

Huck shook his head. "My name is Huck Harrigan, and this is Miss Lavinia McAdams. We're friends. I'm just visiting."

Toby looked from one to the other. "Mr. Huck, Miss Lavinia, can I be your friend, too?"

They each nodded.

Toby's gaze settled on Lavinia. "Good, because I really like you, Miss Lavinia! You're an angel!"

Lavinia's cheeks burned. She was trying desperately to think of a reply when Flora entered the room.

Toby pointed straight at the little girl. "Didn't you say your mama made her best taffy tarts for dessert?"

Flora nodded.

"Can I have one?"

"*May* I have one," she corrected.

"*May* I have one?" he repeated.

"I'll go ask." To Huck and Lavinia, she said, "Mama wants to know if you're coming to the table soon, or if she should put your dinners back in the warming oven."

Huck said, "I think we're done here."

As soon as Flora had delivered a tart to the new Toby, all were gathered together at the dinner table. Huck wasted no time tasting the fish chowder and biscuits and pronouncing them excellent. Then he told Angus, "Our patient let it slip that the biscuits in Marquette don't measure up to your daughter's. He denied he was from there when I asked, but I got the impression that he definitely has connections to the town."

"Marquette, eh?" Angus said thoughtfully. "That's where the Collins and Bancroft furnaces are located. I'll speak with Mr. Harris first thing Monday. He may know someone there."

Mary said, "Meanwhile, the boy will just have to stay with us. Maybe tomorrow, he'll be strong enough to climb the stairs and bed down in Toby's room."

Toby grumbled.

Flora said, "It's going to get awfully confusing with two boys named Toby in the same house."

Mary said, "Then your brother will have to be 'Little Toby' and our guest, 'Big Toby'."

Toby set down his spoon with a clank. "You can't call me Little Toby!"

His mother looked at him in surprise. "Why not?"

"Because I'm going on twelve years old!"

"It's only for a couple of days," Mary assured him, "until Big Toby recovers his strength and moves on."

"Well, I don't like it!"

Angus said, "Would you rather we called you by your middle name, Fergus?"

"Don't call me that!"

"Then you'll have to settle for Little Toby."

With silent resignation, the boy picked up his spoon and returned to his chowder.

The name debate over, Mary said cheerfully, "Monday will be a busy day, now that the slates are here. The children and I will go out, first thing, to call on the youngsters who were interested in learning the three R's."

Lavinia shuddered. Even though she had agreed to help her mother with the tutoring, she dreaded going to visit the shanties, where the street was muddy and the children even muddier.

Angus said, "I have a better idea. Since the furnace is shut down, I'll go with you tomorrow afternoon, soon as you've cleaned up the dinner dishes. The menfolk will be home then—the ones who agreed to enroll their little ones. There's less chance they'll change their minds and turn you away if I'm there with you."

Huck said, "I'll come, too, if you think it will help. I'll admit to arm twisting when I persuaded some of the men to go along with the plan."

Mary said, "Please do come with us! So many of the

shanty folks are new arrivals from your parents' homeland. I'm sure you can speak more eloquently to them than I."

Flora said, "I can hardly wait to go and make some new friends! Now, Mama, may I ask a question?"

"What is it, child?"

"May I bring out your taffy tarts?"

"Yes, dear. Lavinia will help you."

While Lavinia helped Flora in the kitchen, she couldn't help thinking that tonight's dessert promised a far sweeter experience than tomorrow's venture to the shanties.

Chapter

3

Afternoon sunshine broke through the clouds and brightened Lavinia's bedroom, finally making the day worthy of its name, Sunday. Huck would be here at any minute to go with the family to the shanties, and she had come upstairs to brush her hair and put on the scarf and pin that would make her blue dress look special. As she adjusted the scarf around her neck, she could hear Big Toby down in the parlor telling Flora yet another tall tale. Since last evening, he had proven himself a skilled and unrelenting yarn-spinner, and a patient quick to mend as well. Already, he seemed nearly back to full strength, taking meals at the table with the rest of the family and joining in their morning worship service. At first, he annoyed Lavinia, echoing her father's words while he prayed. She wasn't accustomed to two voices praying aloud at the same time, but her father hadn't been the least bit disturbed by it and called it Big Toby's gift of intercessory prayer. They had spent a good amount of time praying for today's outing with Huck. From her window, she could now see him coming up the street.

He was not wearing the dark brown work jacket and shirt she had seen on other occasions, nor was he wearing a cap of any kind. Today he sported a charcoal gray sack suit and white shirt with a stand-up collar and bow tie that made him handsomer than ever. And his red hair shone in the spring sunshine.

Quickly, Lavinia fastened the pewter pin to hold her scarf in place and hurried toward the stairs. Suddenly, she stopped.

No need to rush, she silently chided herself, then slowly proceeded down the steps while Flora answered Huck's knock and invited him in.

Huck had prayed all the way to the McAdams place for a warm reception at each log cabin they would visit today. But most of all, he had prayed for a pleasant time with Lavinia. He didn't know why thoughts of her could stir him so. He only knew that when they were apart, her words echoed uninvited in his ears and the vision of her rare, but enthralling smile flashed unbidden before his eyes.

Now, it was not Lavinia's smile, but little Flora's that welcomed him at the door. He greeted the child with a hug, at the same time glancing beyond the entryway for signs of her older sister. He didn't have to look far. She was descending the stairs, her blue dress lifted just high enough to reveal her dainty ankles. Most impressive of all, though, was the smile that greeted him. For the first time, he sensed that she was truly pleased to see him.

He gazed up at her and smiled in return. "Good afternoon, Miss Lavinia. You're looking especially fine today!"

Lavinia's heart played hopscotch. He hadn't called her "Miss McAdams" as in the past, but the more familiar "Miss Lavinia." And his dark gray suit, drawn taut by his muscular shoulders, made him appear far more attractive up close than at a distance. "You are looking especially fine yourself, Mr. Huck," she replied in kind.

Within moments, all but Big Toby were on the way to the laborers' cabins—Lavinia's father, brother, and Huck leading the way past the hotel toward the muddy street that hugged the shoreline. A gentle breeze warmed by the promise of spring blew in off of Big Bay De Noquette, carrying with it the cries of geese on a northward path and the melodies of sparrows and finches. Lavinia drew in a deep breath, relishing the clean, fresh scent, and the vision of sunlight diamonds that sparkled on the rippled waters.

A little farther on, the pungent smell of wood smoke blended with that of rotting garbage. Barking dogs, grunting pigs, and cackling chickens drowned out the voices of sea- and songbirds, and the shoreline scene of dirty-faced children in filthy clothes suddenly eclipsed the pristine beauty of the bay.

Lavinia lifted her skirt and followed the fellows, her good shoes sinking into the mud. Huck passed the first two cabins, stepping up to the third to knock loudly on the door. A stubble-faced man opened it, releasing the stench of stale cooking grease and a smoldering fire. "Harrigan! Mr. McAdams! What brings you to this neighborhood?"

Huck explained the nature of their mission, then introduced Mr. Reilly to the others. Instantly, he summoned his two children from the dim, dank interior of the cabin, a son, Michael, ten years old, and a daughter, Eileen, who was Flora's age.

Flora greeted her new friend warmly, oblivious of the dirt on her face and the rip in her dress. Michael, though reserved, listened carefully to Mary's instructions concerning time and place for tutoring the next day, and repeated them flawlessly in his Irish brogue.

Mr. Reilly tousled the boy's head. "He is after learning, this one. As for Eileen," his gaze met Mary's, "she's more of a mind to chase after leprechauns than to learn the alphabet, but I've told her she may come to your tutoring sessions so long as she behaves."

"Flora and Lavinia will help her with her letters and

numbers," Mary promised.

Farther up the street, Huck knocked at a cabin identified with the name "O'Connell" over the door. Lavinia was trying to remember why the name seemed familiar when a comely young woman with auburn hair opened the door—the same woman she had run into outside the company store a few weeks earlier. Only today, her dress and apron bore no stains, rather the crisp, clean appearance of fresh laundering and starch.

"Huck Harrigan!" Moira Cleary exclaimed, her blue eyes lighting up her exquisite face. "I pray you've not come for your laundry. I'll have it on Tuesday, as promised." Her lilting words flowed like an Irish melody.

"No, Moira, I'm not here for laundry," Huck assured her, his smile too broad for Lavinia's liking.

A gentleman of short stature, his small sprite of a wife, and their twin girls crowded in beside Moira at the door, the fellow saying, "Do come in!"

Huck and the others stepped just inside the door. While introductions to Moira, Mr. and Mrs. O'Connell, and their eight-year-old twin daughters, Alice and Grace were made all around, Lavinia noticed that this cabin gave a far better impression than the last one. The interior here was plastered and painted white, giving it a fresh, clean appearance. Even the smell was inviting, with a hint of coffee and the aroma of baked goods in the air. She couldn't help noticing that on a blanket in the far corner of the room lay a mongrel nursing four tiny puppies.

The O'Connell twins struck up an instant friendship with Flora, showing her the new litter of pups.

Their father said to Angus, "I do hope you'll stay for coffee. We've a fresh pot."

Moira added, "And my Irish soda bread hot from the

oven."

"That would be—"

Huck finished for Angus. "—a fine idea on such a rare day as this, but we've others to visit, and so we must take our leave."

Moira's smile vanished. "You're sure you won't stay?"

"Not today," Huck said firmly. "Perhaps another time."

Outside, Angus asked Huck, "Why hurry so? I'd have enjoyed a taste of the bread and a cup of the brew."

Huck grinned. "Brew, indeed. I'm given to understand that Paddy O'Connell's Sunday coffee has a bit of Irish lace to it, and not the cotton kind, mind you."

Angus laughed heartily. "Thank goodness you knew that would never do for strict teetotalers like Mary and me."

They continued down the street. Subsequent visits brought introductions to the De Longpre girl, nine, and the Roempke boy, eleven.

They turned toward home, and when they reached the hotel where Huck planned to leave off, Mary said, "Surely you'll come back to the house with us to take tea, won't you?"

Huck glanced Lavinia's way. She offered an irresistible smile. "We have honey and biscuits left from dinner to go with Mama's favorite Darjeeling tea, if you like."

Flora added, "And tarts, too!"

Huck chuckled. "I'd be a fool to turn down such an offer from the three McAdams ladies!"

Conversation resumed in earnest, Mary holding great hope for each scholar's potential, Flora chattering about her newfound friends, Angus and Huck grateful that the men— some of whom had initially opposed the idea—remained steadfast in agreeing to the tutoring of their children. Outside the front door, considerable effort went into cleaning up muddy feet. Upon entering the house, however, attention immediately centered on Big Toby, who lay moaning on the parlor sofa.

Mary rushed to him, placing her hand on his forehead. "What is it, Toby? What's the matter?"

He grimaced, holding his hand against his stomach. "I got a bad bellyache."

"When did it start?"

"A little while after you left," he said with a groan.

Angus said, "We'll get Doc Sloane."

Huck said, "I'll go."

Big Toby protested. "I don't need no doctor!"

Mary told Angus, "He doesn't have a fever. I wonder what it could be?"

"Doc Sloane will figure it out."

Huck said, "I'm on my way."

Little Toby went with him.

Lavinia headed to the kitchen to rekindle the stove fire. While waiting for the tea water to boil, Flora helped her to set out plates, cups, and saucers, but when they folded back the linen napkins covering the basket of biscuits and plate of tarts, disappointment ensued.

Flora stared at the empty plate in disbelief. "Not a crumb!"

Lavinia tipped the bare basket upside down. "Not a crumb here, either!"

The sisters stared at one another.

Lavinia said thoughtfully, "Do you suppose Big Toby's tummy ache . . . "

Flora ran down the hall, braids flying. "Mama! Papa! All the tarts and biscuits are gone!"

Lavinia reached the parlor in time to hear her mother's skeptical reply. "Surely you're joking, child."

"I am not!" Flora insisted. "Tell her, Livvy!"

"It's true, Mama. There's not a crumb to be found."

Mary's brows gathered. "But there must have been at least a dozen tarts and ten biscuits left from dinner."

Big Toby groaned.

Mary pinned a sharp look on him. "Young man, did you eat the tarts and biscuits while we were gone?"

He turned away with a moan.

"Look at me when I'm talking to you, and answer me!"

He gazed up sheepishly. "I'm sorry, Mrs. McAdams."

"Why? Why did you do it?"

Pained, halting words explained. "I got hungry after you left and . . . I was only going to eat one tart but . . . I got started and couldn't stop. Then I ate a biscuit . . ." His moaning resumed.

Angus said, "I want you to tell Doc Sloane the truth when he comes."

"Yes, sir."

Within minutes the doctor arrived and diagnosed Big Toby with a severe case of indigestion. "Time will heal your troubles, young man. From now on, I prescribe no more than one tart and two biscuits at a time. Understand?"

"Yes, sir."

Angus said, "Sorry to disturb you on a Sunday, Doc."

He nodded. "It's a fine day to be out. I took a walk up on the bluff earlier this afternoon. Had my shotgun along in case I came across the fox that's been raiding my chicken coop, and the Harris's."

Lavinia had heard that coops were being raided. Their own chickens had raised a fuss in the middle of the night on more than one occasion, but so far, the fox hadn't been able to penetrate the backyard fence.

The good doctor continued. "I got one shot off, but the

fox scampered away before I could take aim again." He closed up his bag and stood to go. "Fox hunting or no, it's a great day for a walk on the bluff. I'd prescribe it for anyone!"

Lavinia couldn't help noticing Huck glancing her way. While her father saw the doctor out, she returned to the kitchen with her mother and sister to set the tea tray minus biscuits and tarts. With Big Toby occupying the parlor sofa, they decided to serve at the dining table. Little Toby took one sip from his cup and sighed. "If it weren't for Big Toby, we'd all be eating tarts. I sure hate having him around. When's he going to leave?"

Angus said, "Soon, son."

Huck said, "There's an empty bed at the hotel. Seems to me, if Big Toby is up to eating all those tarts and biscuits, he ought to be able to do some chores to earn his keep— once he's over the stomach ache, that is."

"I'll look into it," Angus promised.

Conversation turned to the children that would be gathering around the dining table on the morrow. Flora spoke excitedly of the new friends who would come for the day, and Mary worked out a plan for seating. Teacups drained, Angus offered a prayer of thanks for the time of refreshment and fellowship, and for the new scholars. When he had finished, Little Toby asked Huck, "Do you want to go fishing now?"

Huck shook his head. "Not today, thanks. You see, I was about to ask your father if he would allow me to accompany you and your sisters in fulfilling Dr. Sloane's prescription for a walk on the bluff."

Toby said, "May I, Papa?"

Flora excitedly echoed his plea.

Angus said, "You both may go, if Lavinia goes along to

help look after you."

"*Please,* Lavinia, say you'll go," begged Toby and Flora.

Huck's gaze settled on her, and she knew that the warmth in her cheeks had nothing to do with the hot cup of tea she had just finished. She tossed back her hair. "A walk in the cool air is just what I need. It's a trifle warm in here, don't you think?" She carried her cup, saucer, and spoon into the kitchen, overhearing the words of her father to Huck.

"I expect you to have them all home in one hour. Understand?"

"Yes, sir."

Huck escorted Lavinia out the door behind her brother and sister, who hurried down the street ahead of them. She didn't know why her heart seemed to be racing ahead of her feet or why she was suddenly conscious of everything from the breeze tousling her hair to the dirt-smudged toes of her shoes peeking out from beneath the flounce of her skirt as she walked.

And nothing about Huck escaped her attention, either. His wavy, red hair blew down across his forehead, and he raked it back with his hand. He ran a finger inside his collar, evidently irritated by the tight fit around his thick neck. Then he tugged a tad nervously at the hem of his jacket, and called to Toby and Flora to slow down a tad.

At a comfortable stroll, they followed the youngsters past the wooden frame structure that would soon be the new Town Hall, and the company store, quiet and empty of customers on the Lord's Day. Across from it, wooden uprights marked the site of the Blacksmith Shop that would soon take shape. And to the north stood the furnace, the heart of the town. Its fire was blessedly quiet today, but in Huck's

41

mind, he heard the shouts of men refueling its forty-foot-high, pyramid-like stack with charcoal almost faster than the colliers could provide it. He heard the blasts of hot air fanning the blaze. And he saw molten iron draining out the taphole into channels in the sand floor of the casting house where it formed the bars of pig iron that kept the company going. How much simpler was conversation on a day at the furnace, man-to-man as required by the tasks at hand. But alone with Lavinia, his tongue took on the weight of a 103-pound iron "pig".

Lavinia was rather surprised at the silence of Huck's normally glib tongue, but the lack of conversation allowed for private thoughts—thoughts that raced beyond the charcoal kilns they were now passing and the lime kilns ahead where the children were playing hide and seek. Thoughts that raced up the bluff and continued eastward for hundreds of miles to the Canadian home she had loved and left. Her grandmother's face came unbidden to mind, and the day she waved good bye at the dock. How Lavinia longed to see her again! But the thought vanished from her mind as Toby and Flora met up with her and Huck at the start of the trail. She addressed them sternly. "Toby, Flora, don't run too far ahead. And stay on the trail. Promise?"

"Promise!" they replied, skipping up the path bordered on either side by hardwoods not yet in leaf. Their voices faded as they raced one another to a fallen branch several yards ahead, then teamed up their efforts to drag it out of the way.

Farther along, the trail curved closer to the edge of the bluff, opening up a view of the harbor unobstructed by trees, and furnished with stump seats for resting and taking in the magnificent scene. A few yards ahead, Toby and Flora had found the ideal spot to erect a woodland fort.

Lavinia sat down to take in the sweeping vista that included not only Snail-Shell Harbor, but also the graceful curve of Sand Bay and the point beyond. But it was Fayette that commanded her attention. From here, the charcoal kilns looked like a neat row of toy blocks leading up to a child's model of the furnace with its casting house and stack. The machine shop and the hotel took on a less imposing presence. She could only guess at the location of her own home, and those of the other managers, for they were completely obscured by a grove of trees. But to the north of them, a clearing opened up on a rise. There stood Dr. Sloane's house with its brick ground floor and wooden second story. And beside it rose the most impressive home of all, the superintendent's white house looking out over the harbor that was completely fringed with dock.

Huck perched on a stump near Lavinia who sat chin in hand. He studied her fair, perfect complexion and the tresses of wavy brown hair that adorned her shoulder. He had been to this spot in times past to enjoy the lakeshore view, but it couldn't hold his attention like the girl beside him. She remained deep in thought for several minutes, making him want to inquire concerning her musings, and at the same time, reluctant to intrude. Then, she began to speak, voice quiet, tone contemplative.

"Fayette looks completely different from here." She paused, then went on. "It looks a little more like the place I had in mind when Papa said we were moving to a brand new town in Michigan. I was so excited, I couldn't wait to get here!" She turned to him with a rueful smile. "I had pictured a perfect little village with a church steeple, a school bell tower, and of course, the furnace stack. But when we arrived, Fayette wasn't *at all* what I expected!"

Huck heard bitterness in her words, and saw the moisture welling in her eyes. His heart ached for her.

She swallowed hard and went on. "I never knew how much I would miss Grandma and my friends, and the town where I grew up. I was so homesick at Christmas, the holiday season held no joy at all for me. I would have given anything to be back in Canada! But Mama and Papa said I must stay here until I turn seventeen." She paused a moment, thinking, then continued. "Come the eighth of August, I'm leaving this place. I'm going back to Canada to live with Grandma.

"Of course, Aunt Everilda will be disappointed. She lives in Canada, too. Before we left, she told Mama and Papa that she would love to have me stay with her. She's quite well to do and knows all the right folks. But Aunt Everilda can be very difficult at times. I would much prefer to stay with Grandma Ferguson." She paused, adding, "I really hate this place. I *hate* it!"

Lavinia's words put Huck on notice. Their friendship would be a short one unless her view of Fayette changed. More important was her disappointing Christmas. It reminded him of his own feelings long ago. "I was angry like you on the first Christmas after my folks died."

"How did you manage? How did you ever find happiness again?" Quiet sympathy laced her words.

His head moved slowly from side to side. "For a long time, I didn't. I got angry. I blamed God. I blamed the Captain of the *Augusta*." He explained that in 1860, many Irish, his father included, had joined the Union Guard in Milwaukee. The leaders arranged for a holiday in Chicago aboard the *Lady Elgin*. His folks had died on the return trip to Milwaukee when the *Augusta* rammed her on stormy lake waters. "After that, my older sister and I were sent to live with one aunt and uncle, and my younger brother and sisters went to live with another. It didn't seem fair to be separated from them *and* my folks, but it was the best my relatives could do.

"I had to learn to live in town instead of on the farm. I had to go to school every day instead of down the road to Mrs. Ryan's. I had to get along with a lot of kids I didn't know. And I didn't do very well at it. I was just too angry.

"Then one day I got into a terrible fistfight with one of the boys after school. I punched him as hard as I could right in the nose. He began to bleed. He bled so much, I was sure he was going to die! I was so scared, I ran home and told my Uncle Sean that I'd just killed Big Billy Bassett!"

"Big Billy Bassett?" Lavinia asked, surprise evident on her face.

Huck nodded. "We've known each other for years. After that fight with him, Uncle Sean took me to Billy's house. I was very relieved to see that he wasn't dead. When we got home, my uncle had a long talk with me. He made me see that no amount of anger would bring back Mama and Papa. No amount of anger would unite me with my sisters and brother and put us back on the farm. Then he asked if he could pray for me. We got down on our knees beside my bed and he asked God to help me to make something good of my life. Afterward, I promised Uncle Sean I'd never let anger get the best of me again.

"I really took Uncle Sean's prayer and that promise to heart, and things went better. I stayed out of fights. I finished school and went to work for a carpenter. He was a difficult man and didn't pay much. Then my uncle heard about the jobs at Fayette. He said I could make a better living here if I was willing to work hard, and he offered to pay my way. I told him I'd pay him back. He said that wasn't necessary, but I'm sending him some money each month

45

until I've paid for my passage. It's the least I can do for the man who helped me to make something good of myself."

Lavinia pondered Huck's words. She recalled the night Toby had run out of the house angry, and how he'd returned with a new respect for Huck, his anger gone. "Have you told this to Toby?" she asked.

He nodded.

Now, she understood the change in her brother. She knew, too, the futility of her own anger, having to live in Fayette until her seventeenth birthday. *But how will I stand it here until the eighth of August?*

The question had barely crossed her mind when she realized the woods were too quiet. A glance up the trail revealed an empty fort with no sign of Toby or Flora. Panic sliced through her. "The children! They're gone!"

Huck sprang from his seat and cupped his hands to his mouth. "Toby! Flora!"

Silence answered.

Together, Huck and Lavinia started up the trail, their voices echoing one another.

"Toby! Flora!"

"Toby! Flora!"

From far off came a faint reply.

"Over here!"

Thick undergrowth and low-hanging limbs separated them from the sound. Huck told Lavinia, "Stay here. I'll find them." He veered off the trail, limbs creaking and bushes cracking.

Lavinia watched and listened as Huck disappeared from sight. She could hear him calling out to the children and they continued to answer, but his voice grew ever fainter. Too anxious to stay put, she started after him. Briars snared her skirt, poking holes in the flounce. A low-hanging branch caught her sleeve, ripping it at the shoulder seam. A fallen tree leaned against its neighbor blocking her way. The earth, soft from the rain, held Huck's footprints and she followed them around the obstruction. But before she reached the other side, she stumbled on a vine and fell on her face in the mud.

"I hate this place! I hate it," she repeated bitterly as she picked herself up. Wiping her face with her petticoat, she looked for more footprints, but a thick carpet of leaves offered no hint as to Huck's path.

"Huck! Toby! Flora! Where are you?" she hollered.

Huck's clear voice made reply.

"Over here, Lavinia!"

Pressing past more low branches, she made her way in the direction of his voice, catching a glimpse of three figures in the distance, kneeling in a semi-circle. She hurried ahead, ready to scold Toby and Flora thoroughly for not staying on the trail, and for the dirt smudges and rips ruining their Sunday-best clothes, but the words died in her throat when she saw the object of their attention. There, in a hollow, lay a fox, a gunshot wound in her side, the lifeblood drained out of her while four tiny cubs mewed softly and tried in vain to nurse. She recalled the conversation with Dr. Sloane earlier that day and wondered if this was the creature that he had shot, the fox that had gotten away.

The musk-tinged odor of fox hair and the metallic scent of spilt blood strong in her nostrils, Lavinia reached for one of the cubs, merely a handful of slate-gray fur, and slipped her little finger into its hungry mouth. The wee creature suckled vigorously. "We've got to do something. These babies won't last long without nourishment." She picked up another cub.

47

Toby said, "We could take them home and feed them warm milk."

Huck said, "It will be hard to keep them alive. They're only a few weeks old."

Flora said, "They look almost like the O'Connells' puppies."

Huck snapped his fingers. "That's it! We'll take them to the O'Connells and see if their mama dog will adopt the cubs!"

Lavinia said, "Do you really think she will?"

"It's our best hope," Huck replied. Reaching for the other two cubs, he started toward the trail. "Now let's get back. We're late, and we've got some real explaining to do about your clothes."

Flora hesitated. "But what about the mama fox? Aren't we going to bury her?"

Lavinia said, "Not now, Flora. Come along!"

"But we can't just leave her here!" Flora cried, tears dampening her cheeks.

Huck handed his two cubs to Toby and returned to Flora, kneeling down to take her by the hand. "I promise I'll come back with a shovel and give her a proper burial. Now, will you come with us?"

Reluctantly, she agreed.

Chapter

4

Moira and the O'Connell ladies agreed to take in the cubs and nurse them. When Shamrock refused to accept them, Moira brought out sausage casings she and Alice and Grace had used in the past to nurse abandoned puppies, and filled them with a special formula of warm milk, water, and sugar.

Moira cradled a nursing cub in her arm and pressed between Huck and Lavinia. "The saints be praised, see how this hungry orphan is suckling!"

Lavinia stepped toward the door. "Thank you for your help. Toby, Flora, we'd better get home."

Mrs. O'Connell said, "Promise me now, that you'll take the cubs home once they're weaned."

Mr. O'Connell added, "And when they're grown, you must send them to an island far from shore."

Moira nodded. "Indeed. We've fed enough chickens to the foxes already. Don't need four more raiding our flock."

Flora said, "I promise to take them home as soon as they're old enough. And I promise to come and help nurse them every day, too, when Alice and Grace and I are finished with our lessons." The three new friends beamed with enthusiasm for the plan.

Mr. O'Connell patted Flora's head. "That's a good girl!"

Huck said, "We'll be on our way now. And thanks!"

With a smile and a nod, Mr. O'Connell saw them out.

From the position of the sinking sun and the hands on his pocket watch, Huck knew that the outing to the bluff had far exceeded the one-hour limit set by Angus. He prayed for understanding as his weary band made their way past the hotel and up Stewart Avenue. Nearing the McAdams home, he saw Angus out front watching for their return. Flora darted ahead.

"Papa! Something terrible happened up on the bluff!" Seeing her mother on the doorstep, she ran to hug her. "Mama, it was awful!"

"What, child? Tell me?" Mary begged, but Flora, evidently recalling the dead mama fox, had dissolved in tears, unable to reply as her mother whisked her inside.

Angus took in the others with one swift glance, then his hot gaze settled on Huck, searing through him. "Harrigan, what is the meaning of this, bringing my children home so late, and in such a condition?"

Lavinia spoke up. "It wasn't Huck's fault!"

"Go inside!" he ordered.

"But—"

"You heard me!"

Toby said, "Papa, please listen!"

Angus's gaze bored through him. "Go inside with your sister! Now!"

When they had done as Angus said, he focused on Huck again. Eyes flashing, fists knotted at his sides, he closed within inches of Huck. "What do you have to say for yourself, young man?"

His breath blew hot in Huck's face. He summoned courage to reply. "I—"

"Never mind! Just get out of my sight!" He gesticulated in the direction of the hotel. "I don't want to see you again! Not here, not at the furnace, not ever!"

Huck took a faltering step back, then turned to go. While his feet carried him swiftly toward the hotel, his mind raced in circles. In a single moment his friendship with the McAdams family had been stripped away, and his livelihood, too! It was more than he could comprehend!

Although his afternoon hike in the fresh air had generated an appetite and supper hour was underway at the hotel dining room, he was too upset to eat. He focused instead on the promise he had made to Flora to bury the mama fox. Continuing past the hotel, he returned to the O'Connell cabin to borrow a shovel. When Paddy answered his knock, Huck could see that he had interrupted their meal.

"Sorry to bother you again, Paddy."

Moira was instantly at her brother-in-law's side. "Huck Harrigan! You're just in time for supper!"

Huck shook his head. "Thanks anyway, Moira. It's an Irish spoon I'm after wanting. I promised little Flora that I'd give the vixen a proper burial, and I've got to make haste if I'm to finish before nightfall."

Paddy said, "The shovel's around back. Help yourself."

Moira rested her hand on his arm. "But only if you promise to try my soda bread when you're done with it." Her steadfast gaze defied refusal.

"I'll be back before dark," he promised.

Lavinia had heard her father's angry words to Huck and they plagued her deeply as she helped Flora to wash up and change into her everyday dress. She hated to think that she would never see Huck again. She must find a way to make things right, and fast! She mulled over the problem as she washed the mud off her own face and hands and put on the too-small gray flannel dress she had worn through the winter. With an idea in mind, she turned her attention to the more practical problem at hand, torn and muddy clothes.

With Flora and Toby's help, Lavinia filled a tub with cold water and set their things to soaking. She couldn't help thinking how much work lay ahead, ridding the clothes of their stains and mending the rips and holes. Tomorrow would be a long day. The scholars would come for lessons in the morning and stay until late afternoon. She would walk the children back to the shanty village and check on the fox cubs with Flora. Then she would join the efforts of her mother, brother, and sister, who would already have the laundry chores underway. The younger children would go to bed early, but she and her mother would probably be up until midnight. Even the thought of it made her tired.

While Big Toby continued to recover from indigestion on the parlor sofa, everyone else sat down to a supper of bread and milk. The meal was filled with tense silence until Little Toby set his spoon in his empty bowl and asked his father, "May I please be excused?"

"No, you may not," he replied sternly. "You may wait quietly until the rest of us are finished, and then you and your sisters will explain exactly what happened with Mr. Harrigan on the bluff today."

Toby sighed and slumped in his chair.

"Sit up straight, young man!" Angus demanded.

Toby instantly complied.

Flora cringed.

Lavinia's stomach grew queasy. She'd never seen her father so angry. She forced down the rest of her bread and milk, afraid to leave it lest she be the next to incur her father's wrath. When she had set down her spoon, he said, "Lavinia, you have a lot to explain."

"Yes sir," she replied softly, and began by telling about

the promise the younger children had made to stay on the trail. Then she described the scenic overlook where she sat with Huck to enjoy the view, the fort the children built beside the trail, and the search for Toby and Flora that led to the discovery of the mama fox and four cubs. "The O'Connells' dog refused to adopt the cubs, but Moira and the O'Connell ladies are nursing them with a special formula, and Flora plans to help them every day after school lessons are finished," she concluded.

Angus turned his attention to Toby and Flora. "Did the two of you promise your sister to stay on the trail?"

Both nodded.

"Then why did you break that promise?" he demanded.

Toby said, "It was all Flora's fault! She was pretending to go berry picking! She got lost in the woods and I went to find her!"

Flora argued. "It was your fault, too, Toby! You said you were going hunting so we could have venison for dinner." To her father, she said, "He even carried a stick and pretended it was a rifle. He aimed and shot. Then we heard some crying and found the baby foxes."

Mary said, "You both broke your promise to stay on the trail. In so doing, you worried your sister and ruined your clothes. You both deserve punishment."

Angus said, "Your mother is right. For the next two weeks, Toby and Flora, you may not leave the yard. That means you may not go fishing, Toby. And Flora, you may not go to the O'Connells' to nurse the fox cubs."

"Two weeks?" Toby challenged.

"Hush, or I'll make it four!" Angus warned.

Mary said, "In addition to your school lessons each day, you will memorize the scripture verses I assign you."

Angus's gaze took in all three of his children. "You are

53

all excused from the table. Toby and Flora, you are to go straight to bed."

Lavinia remained seated. She waited until the footsteps of her siblings had reached the second floor, then turned to her father. "Papa, I'm terribly sorry about what happened up on the bluff today. I should have been watching the children more closely. Please don't blame it all on Huck."

"He promised to have you all home in one hour. You were gone nearly two hours!"

"But it wasn't Huck's fault—"

"That's between Huck and me," he said curtly.

Lavinia cast a downward glance at the napkin she was nervously twisting in her hands and silently prayed for guidance. A moment later, when her father's ire had cooled, she looked up at him again. "Papa, there's something I've been meaning all month long to ask you," she said quietly. "Why did you invite Huck here for dinner that first time on April Fool's Day?"

A rueful look troubled his deep blue eyes. "He's different. He's not like the other men who work for the Jackson Iron Company," Angus said thoughtfully. A moment later, he continued. "The other men—even the supervisors—use crude language from time to time. Huck never does. One day I asked him why. He said he loves Jesus too much to curse. Then, I knew he truly was a man of faith so I invited him to supper."

"He's still the same person he was before Toby and Flora ran off in the woods," Lavinia pointed out. "If you're so angry with Huck that you never want to see him again, shouldn't you be just as angry with me? After all, you said I was to look after my brother and sister." Not waiting for a reply, she cleared the dishes from the table and went to the kitchen to help her mother clean up. While washing the dishes, and all throughout the evening, she agonized over Huck's dilemma and prayed for a resolution. It was bad enough that he had been made the recipient of her father's unwarranted anger, but to be dismissed from the furnace as well . . . Troubling thoughts haunted her dreams and disturbed her sleep, leaving her still weary at first morning's light.

Huck rose early with the others on his shift and took breakfast with them in the dining room. But he finished quickly and went back to his quarters alone to pack his belongings, hoping to avoid the others and an explanation for not reporting to the furnace today. Only his good friend, Big Billy Bassett, sensed trouble and followed after him. When Huck finished explaining the circumstances of his dismissal, he said to Billy, "Promise me you won't speak a word of it until the boat from Escanaba has come and gone."

Billy shook his head. "It's not right, McAdams blaming you for the way his kids—"

"Promise me, Billy, not a word!" Huck said again.

After a meditative moment, Billy looked up grinning and threw him a fake right to the side of the head.

Huck sent a series of pulled punches to Billy's gut the way he had on April Fool's Day. Then the whistle at the furnace blew calling the day shift to work.

Billy threw his arms around Huck. "Good luck, you disgrace to ol' Eire, you!"

Huck smiled. "You know I don't believe in luck, Billy. Now get out of here, you son of a sea cook! You'll be late!"

Huck finished packing all his belongings except the laundry still with Moira. Planning to return for it later, he hoisted his small chest to his shoulder, ready to carry it down to the dock, then go in search of the paymaster to give notice he was quitting and make arrangements to collect his wages on the next payday as his contract required. He was headed for the hotel door when Angus McAdams and Big Toby entered. The lad's face lit up.

"Mr. Huck! You're just the fellow Mr. McAdams wants to see!"

Angus offered Huck a stern look. "Get over to the furnace, Harrigan! You're late!"

"But—"

"You heard me! Now get moving, or I'll dock you a half day's pay!"

"Yes, sir!" Huck replied, depositing his trunk in the closest corner of the lobby and heading out the door.

Completely confused by Angus's change of heart, Huck thanked God for this unexpected reversal, then set his mind on his job at the casting house, a stone building with an iron roof that extended for some sixty feet from the side of the furnace stack. Like the other moulders on his crew he took up a heavy sledgehammer and began pounding apart the iron ingots that had been cast at the end of the shift on Saturday. He was thankful that, due to the one-day shutdown they were completely cold now, contributing no additional heat to his sweaty task.

While he labored in the casting house, men were at work above him, charging the stack with tons of charcoal, lime, and iron ore shipped from the Jackson Iron Company mine in Negaunee that would turn into molten metal for the next casting. When Huck and the other moulders had finished breaking apart the iron pigs, they hauled them out of the casting house to stockpiles beside the dock where they would be loaded onto boats for the trip to Cleveland for further refining.

After the cold ingots had all been removed from the casting house, Huck and his crew made ready for the next run-off of molten iron by first dampening the thick layer of sand on the floor with water pumped through a hose. Then they pressed wooden moulds into the sand to form channels to receive the hot iron that would flow from the tap hole. They started with a twenty-foot long "sow" straight down the center. When that main channel was completed, they formed several smaller channels called "pigs" leading off from it in a ladder-like formation. Eventually almost the entire casting house floor had been sculpted to accommodate the smelted iron.

Meanwhile the iron ore inside the furnace had heated sufficiently to melt and flow to the bottom. Only the fire clay plugging the tap hole kept it from escaping. Huck watched as Angus drove the point of an iron bar through the clay plug allowing a shimmering red liquid to flow into the moulds. Fluid fire filled every channel, heating the casting house to an intolerable degree. Huck stepped outside to take a drink of cold water from one of the buckets. Sweat dripped from his brow and dampened his collar, and his arms ached from his morning's labor. Then the whistle marking the midday dinner break sounded, bringing shrill but beautiful music to his ears. He headed for the hotel dining room but had gone no more than two steps when Angus took him aside.

"I pray you'll forgive me for last night. Anger got the best of me and I spoke way out of turn."

Huck nodded. "Forgiven and forgotten, sir."

Angus smiled. "Now go and stoke up. You've got a long afternoon ahead of you."

"Yes, sir!" Huck replied, making haste for the hotel.

At the appointed hour that same morning, the scholars began knocking on the McAdams door. The Reilly children, the De Longpre girl and the Roempke boy were the first to arrive. Lavinia and Flora answered, sending the children straight to the dining room where their mother and Toby assigned seats and passed out slate boards and slate pencils.

The last to arrive were the O'Connell girls accompanied by Moira. When the twins and Flora headed off to the dining room, Moira told Lavinia, "I'll come for the children at noon, and again at the end of the day. What time will they finish?"

"About four. But you needn't come then. I'll walk them home. I've promised my little sister that I'll come to help nurse the fox cubs," Lavinia explained. "Flora would come herself, but Papa has confined her and my brother to the yard for running off in the woods yesterday and coming home with dirty clothes."

"Dirty clothes!" Moira slapped her forehead with the heel of her hand. "I'd nearly forgot! Paddy will be mighty displeased with me if I don't collect your laundry. He's given me strict instructions to do your washing, mending, and ironing in exchange for the tutoring, don't you know?"

"But there's no charge for the tutoring," Lavinia insisted.

Moira waved the notion aside. "Gather your soiled things in a basket for me and I'll be on my way."

Lavinia could hardly believe Moira's generous offer. She hurried to the back yard to collect the clothes that had been soaking over night, then searched the house for the other items in need of washing. She returned to Moira with a large wicker basket mounded high.

Moira accepted it with a smile, balancing it on her hip. "While you were about collecting your things, I remembered that Huck Harrigan told me to be sure and tell Flora that he gave mama fox a decent burial last night." Her smile broadened. "After he finished, Paddy got out his fiddle and me and Huck danced the jig till our feet were sore!" She turned to go. "I'll see you this afternoon, then." As she walked away, she sang a happy tune with such a clear, sweet voice that she put the larks to shame.

Lavinia closed the door, deeply troubled by Moira's words. She had envisioned Huck a distraught man last night, anxious that his job, his home, and his friendships in this town had abruptly come to an end. But such was hardly the case, according to Moira. He hadn't spent the night vexed by misdirected anger and unjust accusations as Lavinia had. Instead, he had danced the night away in the happy company of a very attractive and alluring Irish colleen!

What does it matter? I'll never see him again anyway, Lavinia tried to convince herself. But Moira's words continued to torment her for the rest of the day. They bothered her as she helped Eileen and Michael Reilly to memorize the alphabet, and when she assigned Alice and Grace O'Connell their arithmetic problems.

Unhappy thoughts continued to plague her when she went to nurse the fox cubs, but she was determined not to let it show when the laundress cordially welcomed her inside. Lavinia put forth her best effort to remain friendly, thankful for the toil spared her by Moira.

At home, she helped her mother prepare supper while Toby and Flora memorized Bible verses. When her father returned from his day at the furnace, he went out back to chop wood. A few minutes later, he called Lavinia outside.

59

Pausing to rest, he told her, "I gave a lot of thought to what you said last night, and I want you to know that first thing this morning, I apologized to Huck." He gathered an arm-load of kindling and handed it to her, bending to kiss her on the forehead as he did so. "Thank you for helping me to see the error of my ways. It almost cost me a good friend and employee. Now go back inside and help your mother to get dinner on the table. I've worked up a real appetite for your biscuits!"

Lavinia did as he said, but her mind wasn't on the biscuits and taffy tarts that were baking in the oven or the chicken that was sizzling in the frying pan. Instead, her thoughts vacillated between thankfulness that Huck was still at Fayette and anger over his attention to Moira. When everyone had gathered around the table, her father said a blessing, passed the biscuits and fried chicken, and asked each member of the family in turn about their day. He listened with interest to reports from her mother, Toby, and Flora, of the scholars, and Lavinia's news that Moira Cleary had taken in their laundry. Then, with a big grin on his face he said, "Now, I have an announcement of my own to make. Big Toby has been hired on at the hotel!"

Mary said, "That's wonderful news! What duties will he have?"

"He's to chop wood, wash dishes and the like. In exchange, he gets a bed in the dormitory, three meals a day, and a small allowance."

Toby said, "I hope you told them not to let Big Toby into the pantry."

Angus laughed. "I warned the cook not to leave any leftovers unattended or they may have a very sick fellow on their hands."

Lavinia said, "Did you send a letter off to Marquette?"

Angus nodded. "And I've placed notices in the newspapers there and at Escanaba."

Flora said, "Do you think his mama and papa will come for him?"

"I pray so, Flora, and I hope you will, too," Angus replied.

"I will, Papa, I promise!" Flora assured him.

With the main course over, Mary passed a plate of taffy tarts. Everyone helped himself except Angus, who set the plate aside. His expression turning somber, he said, "Now I have something important to tell you, and I want you all to listen very carefully. I made a big mistake last night, angry at Huck as I was. After hearing you children out about what happened up on the bluff, Lavinia offered me some wisdom of her own. She made me realize that I had blamed Huck in haste. The Bible warns us about anger in Proverbs 14:29. 'He that is slow to wrath is of great understanding; but he that is hasty of spirit exalteth folly.' Don't give way to quick anger, children. It only leads to regret."

After a moment's reflection, Flora said, "Papa, does this mean you're going to be punished?"

Toby said, "Flora, you don't know anything. Papa only *gives out* punishment. He never *gets* punished."

Angus shook his head. "Toby, you couldn't be more wrong. I don't expect you'll understand till you're grown up, but I've been punished for my quick temper. I lost a good night's sleep last night. And while you all have been eating your mother's taffy tarts, I've been eating humble pie." A knock sounded at the door and Angus said, "That's Huck. I promised I'd go fishing with him after supper."

Toby started to get up. "I'll let him in."

Flora said, "Let *me* do it!"

Angus said, "Stay put, you two. Your sister will go."

61

To Lavinia, he said, "Please tell Huck I'll be right there."

Reluctantly, she headed for the front door. A thought coming to her, she opened it with a broad grin. "Well, if it isn't Huck Harrigan! I'm surprised you made it all the way here from the hotel, I am."

Bewildered by Lavinia's manner of speech, and her words, he asked, "Are you all right?"

"That I am, but you must be suffering from an acute case of tired feet after dancing the night away with Moira Cleary."

Huck's cheeks glowed like a double crimson sunset.

"Papa will be here in a minute," she said curtly, turning to walk away.

He stopped her, his hand on her arm. "Lavinia, you don't understand!"

Jerking free, she replied, *"You're* the one who doesn't understand!" Heels clicking, she disappeared down the hall.

Chapter
5

The following day, when Lavinia walked home with the O'Connell twins to check on the fox cubs, Moira presented her with a laundry basket full of clean, pressed clothes. Thanking her with genuine gratitude, Lavinia carried the load home, inspecting each piece as she put it away, paying particular notice to the clothing damaged on Sunday's walk to the bluff. Much to her surprise, the rips and holes were nearly indistinguishable, and the stains had completely vanished. Thankful to have her blue dress back, she took off the ill-fitting gray one.

But the change in outward appearance could not alter her melancholy heart, blue as the dress she now wore. She was no match for the Irish colleen of comely face, songbird voice, dancing feet, and magic needle.

From the bottom of the stairs, her mother's voice floated up to her. "Lavinia, I need your help in the kitchen."

"Coming, Mama."

Folding her gray dress, she lay it carefully in her trunk, wishing she could as easily lay aside her feelings for Huck Harrigan.

Huck folded the page, placed it in the envelope, and addressed it to his Uncle Sean. He'd be pleased to hear that all was going well at the furnace. Huck only wished his friendship with Lavinia would run as smoothly as the molten iron when it poured into the casting house. Instead, his evening at the O'Connells' had acted as a fireplug, damming the flow. Somehow, he must find a way to break out the plug, and he must do it soon. Come August 8, Miss Lavinia McAdams would be on a boat to Canada unless he gave her reason to stay in Fayette.

Huck stood up, slid the letter into his pocket, and headed for the business office, gold coins jingling in his pocket as he went. At least he was making progress in repaying his debt of honor to his uncle. By year's end, he'd have his passage to Fayette repaid in full. Then, if Lavinia would have him, he could afford to make her his wife. But for now, he was content to be sending a draft to his Uncle Sean for as much as he could spare from this month's pay.

The week passed, and then another. After a rainy Saturday night, Sunday morning dawned cloudy but dry, and Lavinia couldn't remember ever being more thankful to put aside old troubles and start anew. Memories of the previous several days haunted her as she brushed her hair. Huck had come several times to go fishing with her father, but she managed to avoid him completely.

She had walked the O'Connell children home from tutoring sessions daily, encountering the inimitable Moira each time. The laundress had treated her with unfailing cordiality and respect, making her difficult to dislike. Her kindness acted as a double-edged sword. As hard as Lavinia tried to dislike the Irish colleen, she couldn't. And when she tried to convince herself that Moira was unsuitable for Huck, she only succeeded in doing the opposite.

When three of the fox cubs died, Moira even wrapped them in burlap so Lavinia could take them home for a proper back yard burial. The loss of the cubs had placed a special burden of grief on little Flora who felt personally responsible, because she had been restricted to the yard and unable to help nurse the creatures herself.

As Lavinia arranged her scarf about her neck and fastened it with the pewter pin, she was thankful that the furnace had shut down last night until the hearth could be replaced, allowing her father another rare opportunity to enjoy the entire Sabbath with the rest of the family. And she was thankful, too, that Toby and Flora's restriction to the yard would likely be lifted today. When she arrived at the breakfast table, she saw that the long faces her brother and sister had worn for two weeks had been replaced by smiles.

By the time the breakfast dishes were cleared, Big Toby had come knocking on the door, asking to join the family worship service. When Angus welcomed him heartily, the boy hurried into the dining room, stood at the foot of the table with a big smile on his face, and said, "Guess what happened to me last night!"

Little Toby said, "You ate a whole pie for dessert."

Big Toby frowned. "You're wrong. Guess again!"

Angus said, "It must have been something good."

Big Toby nodded. "Guess!"

Flora said, "Did you make a new friend?"

Big Toby shook his head. "I'm already friends with everybody at the hotel."

Angus said, "Why don't you sit down and tell us what happened."

He took a place beside Angus and began to talk in earnest. "You know my boss, Mr. Rose? Well last night after I finished work, he said he wanted to see me in his office. I was scared. I thought I'd done something wrong and he was going to yell at me, so I said, 'I haven't done anything wrong, Mr. Rose. Honest I haven't!' And he said, 'I know you haven't done anything wrong. You're a real hard worker, one of the best I've ever seen. I'm going to give you a raise. Starting next week you're going to earn two cents more every day.' Think of all the candy I could buy over at the company store with two cents more every day!"

Mary said, "Are you sure you should spend all that money on candy every month?"

Lavinia said, "It would probably make you sick like the time you ate all those biscuits and tarts."

Angus said, "Maybe you should ask God what to do with the extra money when we have our prayer this morning."

Big Toby's brow furrowed and after a moment's thought, his smile returned. "You're right, Mr. McAdams, I'll ask God about it."

Angus said, "Let's join hands and each of us will pray according to our need, beginning with Big Toby."

When heads were bowed, Big Toby said, "Almighty God, thank you for the raise from Mr. Rose. Please tell me how to spend the money, and please let me buy at least one piece of candy each week with it."

The prayer continued with Flora and Little Toby each praying that they had been obedient enough for their father to lift their restrictions now that their two weeks of confinement had lapsed. Angus prayed for a church and school to be erected soon in the village, and Mary prayed for more books and supplies for the scholars coming each day for tutoring. Lavinia considered praying for someone from Big Toby's family to reply to her father's letter to Marquette or the newspaper notices there or at Escanaba that had thus far gone unanswered. But with the boy so happy in his work at the hotel, it seemed a shame that he might be taken away from it, so instead she prayed for news from her grandmother.

When her "Amen" had been said, Big Toby lifted his head and stated firmly, "I know what God wants me to do with my raise!" Turning to Angus, he said, "He wants me to give half of it to you for a new church building!"

Angus beamed. "Praise God! If everyone else in the village would be as obedient as you, we'd have a church built in no time!"

Little Toby's gaze met Big Toby's. "What does God want you to do with the other half? Did He tell you to give it to me?"

Big Toby scowled and shook his head vigorously. A grin returning, he said, "God told me it was all right to buy candy with it as long as I don't eat more than one piece a day."

Mary said, "Praise be! Self-restraint is an important virtue, Big Toby. God will bless you for it."

When the family worship service ended, Big Toby returned to his duties at the hotel, and Lavinia and Flora helped their mother prepare the midday meal. At the dinner table, Little Toby and Flora, still in hopes of having their restrictions lifted, behaved like model children. When the dessert of vanilla custard had been enjoyed and they asked to be excused, Angus said, "You may leave the table after you answer one question. What lessons have you learned during your confinement to the yard?" After a silent moment while the children stared at their laps, he said, "Toby, you will answer first."

The young boy lifted his gaze. "It's no fun staying home and helping Mama while you go fishing. I shouldn't have run off in the woods."

"Flora?"

"I wish I'd never run off in the woods. I wish we'd never found those fox cubs!" Tears glazed her eyes.

Angus spoke tenderly. "Dearest Flora, we told you before, it wasn't your fault that three of them died. Besides, one of them is still alive and healthy. Wouldn't you like to go and see it today?"

"May I?" she asked tentatively.

"You may, as long as your mother or sister goes with you." Angus replied. "You and Toby are no longer restricted to the yard."

Toby's face beamed. "Does that mean I can go fishing now?"

Angus put his napkin aside. "Let's go together, son!"

Flora turned excitedly to her sister. "Livvy, you'll take me to O'Connells', won't you? *Please!*"

"Of course I will," she agreed despite her reluctance to encounter Moira again.

Mary said, "All three of us will go as soon as we finish with the dishes."

By the time they left for the O'Connells', clouds had given way to full sun. When they arrived, Lavinia noticed that several half-peck baskets stood in a stack just inside the door. Flora scampered across the room, ignoring Shamrock and the puppies tumbling and tussling at her side, to the blanket where her fox cub lay. Carefully picking it up, Flora cuddled and stroked it, her face beaming.

Moira said, "I do believe that one will live. Have you settled on a name?"

"Cubby!" Flora replied.

Mr. O'Connell chuckled. "That's an apt name, if ever I heard one."

While Flora, Alice, and Grace played with the cub and

puppies, Mrs. O'Connell told Mary and Lavinia, "We ladies are going up Furnace Hill to the woods to gather mushrooms this afternoon. After last night's rain, I expect a new crop has sprung up. Come with us, won't you?"

Mary turned to Lavinia. "It's up to you."

Moira, said, "Come! And tonight you'll feast on mushrooms fit for the saints!"

Lavinia laughed. "I hardly qualify, but I'd like to go— if you'll allow me time to change my dress. I'd hate to ruin this one a second time in the woods."

Mary said, "Flora and I must change, too. And we'll leave a note for Papa, and fetch our baskets."

Mrs. O'Connell said, "We'll meet up with you shortly, in front of the furnace."

When Lavinia arrived at the furnace with her mother and sister, she noticed that not only were Moira and the O'Connell ladies waiting there, but also Big Billy Bassett. He carried Moira's basket on the trek up Furnace Hill and seemed never to take his gaze off her. While Moira and the O'Connells sang *Green Bushes* and taught the verses to Lavinia, her mother, and sister, Big Billy followed quietly along, his expression never changing from a look of admiration that curved his mouth gently upward.

Lavinia's attention, consumed by the song and her observations of Big Billy and Moira at first, gradually shifted to the change that had settled in upon the woods surrounding Fayette. No longer were they the dreary and foreboding place of two weeks ago. With the unfolding of spring, so had a wildflower carpet unfolded on the woodland floor. Trees still bare of leaves had become an enchanted forest. When Mrs. O'Connell stepped off the road, Lavinia imagined herself transported to some sort of fairytale world. As far as the eye could see, white, three-petal flowers with vibrant green leaves had sprung up to hide the drab fallen leaves. Lavinia couldn't resist the bright little jewels, stooping to pick blossom after blossom until her basket was half full.

When Mrs. O'Connell saw what she had done, she laughed. "From the looks of your basket, it's trillium soup you'll be eating tonight!" Stooping beside a fallen tree, she pressed aside dead leaves and emerald green foliage to reveal a collection of small, cone-shaped mushrooms with sponge-like caps. "These are what we're after—morels. Mm. I can taste them already!" She pinched off the stems at ground level, explaining that by leaving part of the mushroom in the soil, more would grow in years to come, and that they most often sprang up at the foot of decaying trees, especially elm trees.

Lavinia began looking for the elusive morels in earnest, discouraged by their ability to hide beneath fallen leaves. She hummed as she went, stooping often to brush away a layer of debris only to find barren soil. But she pressed ahead, so focused on the hunt for mushroom treasures that when she encountered a pair of men's boots on the feet of someone standing in front of her she shrieked, falling back to land on her fanny!

Huck's voice offered reassurance, as did the hands he extended. "I'm sorry, Lavinia, I didn't mean to startle you."

She looked up to find a smile broad as Snail-Shell Harbor on his face. A short distance away, she heard Moira, Billy, and the others chuckling. Laughing at herself, she accepted Huck's helping hands. Once on her feet, she attempted to release herself to retrieve her basket, but he wouldn't let her go. Instead, he entwined his fingers with hers, sending a warmth through her that was enhanced by the gaze of his admiring blue eyes.

"You've been avoiding me for two weeks," he gently accused.

Casting a fleeting glance in the direction of Moira and Billy, she turned again to Huck with a grin. "Silly of me, wasn't it?"

"Silly indeed, since Moira's only interest in me was due to my friendship with Billy," Huck quietly explained. Releasing one of her hands to pick up her basket, he kept her other hand firmly in his and walked on.

With Huck's hand tightly holding hers and the hunt for mushrooms continuing in the enchanted forest, Lavinia couldn't help thinking of the girl after which she was named. "Have you ever read a poem called 'Seasons' by James Thomson?"

Huck shook his head.

"Have you ever read about Ruth and Boaz in the Bible?"

"Once or twice," Huck replied, aware that it was a story of a girl gleaning in a field, and that she eventually married the owner of the field.

Lavinia continued. "Then you'll understand the 'Autumn' section of Thomson's poem about Palemon and Lavinia. It's a love story like Ruth and Boaz. I can imagine my namesake in the spring of the year walking through an enchanted forest like this, hunting for mushrooms for her and her penniless mother. She's having no success at all when along comes a handsome fellow on a white steed. Her face seems familiar to him, and upon inquiry he discovers that she is the daughter of his friend of long ago, the one who sold him the forest. For years he had been searching for her in vain, but now he has finally found her and rescues her from a life of drudgery and penury."

Huck paused, turning to face Lavinia. His hand still holding hers, his countenance solemn, he said, "I'm glad you're not living a life of drudgery and penury, but if you were, I would surely want to be the wealthy landowner who comes to rescue you." After a moment's reflection, his mouth curved upward. "Would a pig iron man from Wisconsin do?"

Lavinia gazed at him in silence, enjoying the fantasy of Huck as her landowner rescuer. But suddenly the enchanted forest had turned back into the woods up the road from the furnace. With all her heart she wanted Huck to be her hero, while her head told her she did not want to live the rest of her life in the shadow of a furnace stack. Summoning a modest smile, she replied, "As my Grandma Ferguson always says, only time will tell."

Huck released Lavinia's hand and resumed the hunt for mushrooms, pressing leaves aside with the toe of his boot to uncover a patch of morels, tiny and fresh. As they harvested the little jewels, he silently berated himself for pressing Lavinia as he had. Their friendship was still new, their feelings untested. Like it or not, Lavinia was right—only time would tell. But time was too short. She was so adept at avoiding him for weeks at a stretch that he would never be able to capture her affections before the eighth of August. Even if he *could*, what then? He had no extra money for courting or future plans, not while he still had his debt of honor. Repaying his uncle the money borrowed for passage to Fayette came first.

Lavinia sensed a quiet reserve in Huck as they continued their search for mushrooms. Each time they stooped to pick a cluster of hidden sponge caps, her hand brushed against his, yet he made no attempt to entwine his fingers with hers. Nor did he hold her hand when they headed back down the road toward town behind the others, their basket brimming.

When they arrived outside Lavinia's front door, Huck handed her the basket. "I've got to get back. It's nearly supper hour at the hotel."

"But I thought you would be staying for cream of mushroom soup," Lavinia protested.

Huck shook his head. "Some other time, thanks anyway." He turned and headed toward town without so much as a wave good bye.

She went inside, closing the door a little more firmly than usual. Seeing that her mother and Flora were already at the well in the back yard pumping water into a bucket to wash their mushrooms, she joined them there. Adding her own to their slim pickings, she began gently swirling them around to release the dirt and bugs. She could sense her mother's gaze on her and the question that was about to come. She wasn't disappointed.

"Where's Huck?"

"He went back to the hotel," Lavinia quietly replied.

Flora said, "I was so sure he'd stay for supper!"

"Maybe he doesn't like mushroom soup," Lavinia suggested, even though she was fairly certain it wasn't the soup he disliked. She wondered if she would see him again, or if a chill even colder than the well water now numbing her hand had settled over their friendship forever. She was mulling over the frigid notion when the voices of her brother and father interrupted her thoughts.

"Mama, look at this!"

"Lavinia! Flora! Look at your brother's fish!"

Lavinia turned to see her brother toting a huge trout into the back yard with the help of his father.

Mary's eyes opened wide. "Toby! I can't believe it!

73

That fish must weigh . . . "

Angus finished for her. "Twenty pounds, at least!"

Lavinia said, "It's a third as heavy as Toby!"

Flora said, "Are you going to cook it for supper, Papa?"

"Not me!" Angus replied. "Toby, tell your mother and sisters what happened when we were fishing at the dock."

Toby said, "We hadn't been there long when Mr. Harris and his son, George, came by. They started fishing, and weren't getting many bites. When I caught this huge trout, Mr. Harris asked if we'd all like to come up to his place for a fish fry. We're headed up there now to clean this big fellow."

Mary said, "Do you suppose the Harris's would like some mushrooms to fry with that fish? We've been gathering them in the woods all afternoon. They'll never taste better than they will tonight."

Angus reached for the bucket. "I'm sure Mr. Harris's cook will be delighted with your mushrooms. Now come along, ladies!"

Mary protested. "I look a fright! I'll be along as soon as I put on my Sunday dress."

Lavinia said, "I need to change, too."

Flora said, "Me, too."

Angus said, "I'll tell the Harris's you'll be along in a few minutes."

As Lavinia changed from her old gray dress to her favorite blue one, she knew she should be thrilled with the invitation to the big white house on the hill. Instead, she couldn't help thinking that the one person she wanted to sup with would not be there.

Chapter 6

Huck claimed his customary place at the hotel dining table just as the meal was being served. When he saw and smelled the slice of squirrel pie on his plate, he regretted keenly turning down both of the invitations he'd received to join the McAdams family for supper. After refusing Lavinia, he had met Little Toby and Angus heading home with a huge trout and they had invited him to come along to the Harris's for a fish fry, but again he had declined. Lifting his fork, he cut into the stubborn crust of the squirrel pie. The morsel of meat he gathered with it on his fork proved to be chewy and unsavory, and the gravy was greasy, but no one else seemed to notice. The other fellows were in too good a humor after patronizing the illegal trade in alcohol offered by boats that came calling at Sand Bay half a mile south of the hotel. The cook could have served them three-day-old fish and they probably wouldn't have noticed.

Leaving his portion uneaten, Huck slipped away from the table and headed toward the docks. Sitting down at the edge of the harbor with the fresh breeze blowing against his cheeks and the sun shining warm upon his face, he pondered the afternoon's events. In Lavinia's company, time had passed quickly and pleasantly until she had spoken those four words that had settled in his mind to haunt him mercilessly. *Only time will tell.*

The phrase was a cutting reminder that while his feelings for her were like iron from the furnace, warm and glowing, her feelings for him were more akin to the iron ore in the charge. It had yet to melt and mingle with the flux that would carry away doubt like so much slag. Reluctantly, he reminded himself that Lavinia's grandmother was right. In many questions of life only time will tell, and the bonds of affection that he longed to form with Lavinia were no exception.

He gazed out across the waters. A boat was headed for Snail-Shell Harbor, a schooner that looked like thousands of others on the lakes. Within minutes it came alongside the dock. He scrambled to catch the bowline tossed by the mate. Tying it securely, he ran to catch the stern line, wrapping it around the piling until the vessel was snug against its bumpers. A crewman bounded onto the dock, setting a ramp in place, then helping an elderly woman to disembark. Once on the dock, she lifted her gaze to meet Huck's, a very becoming and seemingly familiar smile on her face.

"You wouldn't know the McAdams clan that lives hereabouts, would you, son? I'm in search of Angus and Mary—she's my daughter."

"I know the McAdams clan well," Huck replied, suddenly aware that this was the grandmother of whom Lavinia had spoken so fondly.

"I'd be most obliged if you'd direct me to their lodgings."

"I'll do better than that," he offered. "I'll take you to the McAdams's myself."

The crewmen deposited two large trunks beside the woman, prompting Huck to ask, "Will you be staying long?"

She shrugged. "Only time will tell. But between you, me, and that gull up there, now that I'm here I'm in high

hopes of putting these old trunks into permanent retire-
ment."

Huck smiled, silently praying that such would be the
case, and that Lavinia's keen longing for Canada would
fade now that her beloved grandmother had arrived.

Lavinia had been to the Harris home briefly last
December for wassail and cookies, but this was the first
time she had been invited to the white house for a meal.
She was looking forward to seeing what the previously
unfinished dining room looked like now that Mrs. Harris
would have had time to choose wallpaper and furnishings,
but instead the meal was served on a picnic table in the yard
overlooking the harbor and furnace. After everyone had
been seated, including Marian Phillip, a hired servant of
about twenty-five years in age, Angus asked a blessing.

Joseph Harris echoed the "Amen" then gazed out at the
harbor and town, a satisfied smile creasing his ruddy face.
With a sweeping motion of his thick arm, he remarked,
"This is the best 'dining room' on all of Lake Michigan,
don't you agree, McAdams?"

"None better, I presume," Angus replied.

Mrs. Harris passed the platter of fish to Lavinia's mother, saying, "Joseph is always thinking of ways to get George
and me outside for a meal." She shooed away a pesky fly.
"Truthfully, I prefer the dining room where the pests aren't
so prevalent."

"What's a fly or two, Harriet, when the full pleasure of
a fine spring day in the great outdoors is yours for the taking, along with a view unmatched in all of Northern
Michigan?" With the flick of his hand he caught a fly in
mid-air, then tossed it lifeless to the ground.

Suddenly, George pointed to the harbor entrance.

"Papa, look! A boat is coming in!"

Joseph gazed intently, studying the craft. "It's not one of ours," he said, referring to the Jackson Iron Company fleet. "I wonder who it could be?"

George started to rise. "Toby and I will go find out for you, Papa."

Joseph raised his palm. "Stay put. Eat your fish. We'll know soon enough." To Harriet, he said, "Pass those mushrooms, will you, dear? I'm eager to give the McAdams ladies' specialty a try."

He passed the plate on to Lavinia who added a few mushrooms to the small portion of fish on her plate. One taste had her wishing she'd taken more. The breaded coating Marian had added substantially enhanced the flavor and texture of the delicate morels.

While Lavinia savored the mushrooms, and the flaky tenderness of Toby's lake trout, talk flowed freely for several minutes of the Harris family's former experiences at the Morgan, Bancroft, and Greenwood furnaces in Marquette County, and her own family's hometown in Canada. When the topic turned to Fayette, Harriet expressed her admiration for the tutoring Mary had taken up to help the immigrant children.

"I could no more teach a roomful of youngsters than I could smelt a ton of iron. It's all I can do to keep my own son at his studies for an hour or two each day."

The rattle of a wagon pulling into the driveway commanded the attention of all. Lavinia was surprised to see Huck and Big Toby occupying either end of the driver's bench, and when she saw who was sandwiched between them, her jaw went slack.

Mary gasped with delight, then hurried to greet the elderly woman being helped down by Huck and Big Toby.

"Mama! I can't believe it's you!"

Little Toby ran to his grandmother, followed by Flora and Lavinia, one gleeful word on their tongues.

"Grandma!"

Angus joined the others. After hugs and kisses had been exchanged all around, questions flowed from Mary, Lavinia, and her father in a torrent.

"When did you get here?"

"*How* did you get here?"

"Why didn't you tell us you were coming?"

Grandma replied rapidly. "'Twasn't time for a letter, and 'twasn't more than a few minutes ago that I got off the boat. These two young fellows, here, offered to bring my trunks and me up from the dock." She smiled appreciatively at Huck and Big Toby.

Huck's gaze caught and held Lavinia's for an instant.

She offered him a smile of thanks then hugged her grandmother again. "I still can't believe you're here, Grandma!"

Big Toby said, "I don't know why you're so surprised to see your grandma, Miss Lavinia. Didn't you pray for it this morning?"

His words gave her pause. "Yes, but I didn't expect an answer so quickly."

Angus said, "Let this be a lesson to all. Never underestimate the power of prayer!"

Mrs. Harris approached, her hand extended to the elderly woman. "I'm Harriet Harris. Would you like to join us for supper? We've plenty of trout and mushrooms, thanks to the generosity of your kin, here. And Marian has yet to serve up the spice cake."

"I'd be most appreciative. I haven't had a decent meal since breakfast."

As the others headed toward the picnic table, Lavinia lingered, her attention on Huck and Big Toby. "Thank you for bringing Grandma up here."

Huck gave a nod and a smile.

Big Toby said, "Our pleasure, Miss Lavinia. We'll leave her trunks at your folks' place on our way back to the hotel."

Impulsively, Lavinia hugged Big Toby and kissed his cheek, then did the same with Huck.

His arms went tentatively around her. Then the embrace ended all too quickly. But the feeling lingered, of her soft warmth pressed gently against him. The sensation carried him on a cloud above the driver's seat while descending the hill to the McAdams's place. There, he and Big Toby carried two large, heavy trunks from the wagon into the front hall, then returned to the hotel to unhitch the team.

His heart still soaring on an invisible cloud in a sky of pure blue, Huck wandered toward the dock again, all the while trying to warn himself that Lavinia's show of affection was strictly impulsive, borne of happiness at reuniting with her grandmother. After all, she gave Big Toby a kiss and hug, too. But he ignored that fact to focus on a happier one. The grandmother Lavinia had missed so dearly had come to Fayette, ready to settle in. Lavinia's most important reason for returning to Canada was now her most important reason for remaining at Fayette. Such knowledge made his spirits soar like sparks from a newly charged furnace aglow with the promise of a solid and productive future.

Grandma Ferguson deferred a discussion of her trip saying she was too hungry to talk. When she had eaten her fill of the trout and mushrooms and everyone had been served

80

a piece of spice cake, Lavinia pursued the subject.

"Now tell us all about your trip from Canada, Grandma!"

"It's a frightfully long story. I hate to impose it upon our hosts." She turned to Harriet. "You've been most gracious, already."

"We're all eager to hear of your travels," Harriet assured her with a smile.

"Well, then, I'll start with the morning I crossed over to Detroit. It didn't take me long to find a schooner heading this way, so I booked a cabin and soon we were in tow up the river, across the St. Claire Flats, and up to Port Huron. We left there early in the morning along with several other vessels, then a gale blew in from the northwest and the waves began to roll. Uuup and down, uuup and down." Her gaze landed on Toby.

"How big were they, Grandma?" He asked eagerly.

Her brow furrowed, resembling a whitecap. "I don't rightly know, Toby. I was down in my cabin and didn't get a good look at them. But from the feel of it, I'd say they were higher than a wood shed but smaller than a barn. Anyway, the crew had a tough time of it, getting the boat turned around, but eventually, we headed back. Then the captain saw a boat that was in real trouble—a prop. boat." She referred to a propeller-driven steamer. "And before our captain's very eyes, that boat's smokestack toppled and fell. I heard tell later that when the steamer had tried to turn back, it got caught in a swell that took half the wheelhouse overboard along with the helmsman. Then water poured into her and doused her furnaces, and finally she sank, spilling thirty-three passengers and twenty-one crew into the foamy waves with her."

Flora's eyes grew wide. "You mean all those folks

drowned?"

"Nearly all," her grandmother said solemnly. "Now, the wreck was only a half mile away from us, so our captain steered for it to see if he could pick up any survivors. He took on but one man, the first engineer. The poor fellow was suffering badly from immersion and shock, and as soon as we got back to Port Huron, he went straight to the hospital. Reporters and insurance men descended on our captain and took his account of what he'd seen. The helmsman was so sick, they thought he might die before he could tell what had happened." She paused to smile. "I'm pleased to say that the rest of the trip was rather tame compared to that gale. I don't think my nerves could have stood another such storm." She described a calm trip up Lake Huron, the thick fog that threatened to ground them near the Straits of Mackinac, and the pleasant sail from there to Fayette.

Her traveling tales finished, she thanked the Harris's once again for their hospitality. Then Lavinia slipped her arm through her grandmother's for the short walk home.

When Mary saw her mother's two trunks in the hallway, she said, "Angus, Lavinia, please help me rearrange the furniture in the parlor, will you? We need to make a place for Mother's trunks so she can use the room as her bedroom." To Flora and Toby, she said, "Please fetch your grandmother some sheets and blankets for the sofa—and a pillow, too." She turned to her mother. "I'm sorry for the bare window. I've been meaning to order curtains. Maybe I can find an old sheet so you'll at least have some privacy."

"No need," Grandma insisted. Opening one of her trunks, she pulled out a bundle of lace, unfolding it to reveal a pair of curtains. "These ought to do, don't you think?"

Mary gasped with delight. "They're perfect! Thank you, Mother!"

Lavinia helped hang the curtains, noticing a certain familiarity about them. "These look exactly like the lace curtains in *your* parlor, Grandma."

"So they do," she replied, continuing with her unpacking.

When the room had been rearranged and furnished with a ewer and basin, and towel and soap, Grandma said, "It's been a long day, and I'm weary to the bone. I think I'll wash up and turn in, if you don't mind."

Mary hugged her mother. "Good night. I'll see you in the morning."

When Toby, Flora, and Lavinia had kissed their grandmother good night, Mary said, "Children, it's been a long day for all of us. It's time for you three to go up to bed. Your father and I are turning in now, too.

Lavinia's dreams were filled with the images of her grandmother's trip—the storm of Lake Huron, the fog of the straits, and the calm waters to Fayette. They were filled, too, with the image of Huck, and the feel of his arms gently around her when she kissed him in thanks for bringing her grandmother up to the Harris's. The sense of him was so strong, she thought she was actually with him again, pressed against his broad, strong chest, taking in the manly scent of him. Then she awoke and realized she had only been with him in a dream this time.

Pleasant memories filling her mind, she soon drifted off to sleep again. She slept soundly and woke early to the smell of coffee and bacon, and the intermingling of her mother's, father's, and grandmother's voices. While Flora and Toby slept on, she dressed and headed downstairs. She overheard her grandmother's words as she entered the dining room.

"When the fire burned their house down, I never suspected that soon *I'd* be the one without a home."

Lavinia's mother greeted her with a smile. "Good morning, dear! I have eggs and bacon in the warming oven. Would you care for some?"

"Yes, please." While her mother went to fetch her breakfast, Lavinia kissed her grandmother on the cheek and took the place beside her. "Good morning, Grandma! It's so good to have you at our table!"

"Good morning, dear! It's a blessing to be here, believe you me!"

Angus said, "Your grandmother was just telling your mother and me about your Uncle John and Aunt Lucinda, and Jack and Lucy." He named Mary's younger brother, the black sheep of the family, and his difficult wife and their unruly children. "They lost their home in a fire and moved in with your grandmother last January."

Lavinia said, "I'm sorry to hear it."

Her grandmother said, "Not half as sorry as I, I'll tell you. They came to my door with nothing but the clothes on their backs, a pitiful sight on a cold winter's night. Naturally, I told them they could stay with me a while. Little did I suspect that once they settled in, they would decide there was no point in rebuilding when they could just take over the family home."

Mary set a plate in front of Lavinia and returned to her place. "John has had his share of difficulties, but I—"

Her mother interrupted. "Difficulties he's brought on by being such a cantankerous soul!"

Mary continued. "Even so, I never thought my brother would purposely make you so miserable you'd be eager to move out of the house Papa built for you. I know how you love the grove of maples that surround the place, and that special stained glass window in the breakfast nook with the maple leaf in the center that catches the morning sun." She shook her head in disbelief. "To think John made matters so difficult that you would leave it all behind."

"All but my lace curtains!" Grandma claimed, her eyes twinkling.

Lavinia laughed. "So those *were* the curtains from your parlor."

"The very same. I could see no point leaving them on the windows for that ungrateful lot when your mother had need of them."

Mary shook her head in sad disbelief. "I certainly underestimated John's dark side."

Grandma said, "I share the very same fault. I can see now that I myself underestimated your brother's dark side by several shades of black. One day he'll pay dearly for the trouble he's caused." She paused to sip her tea. "But I'm here now, and glad to be. I'll help with the cooking and the washing and the children and anything else that needs doing. I'm determined not to be an imposition."

Lavinia set down her fork and turned to her grandmother in earnest. "You could never be an imposition!"

The elderly woman took Lavinia's hand in her own, giving an affectionate squeeze. "I hope not, dear. Now, if you'll excuse me a minute, I need to fetch something from my trunk."

Lavinia exchanged curious glances with her folks. Moments later, her grandmother returned to set a small tin box on the table beside her father.

"Son, this is all I have to my name aside from the personal possessions contained in my trunks. If you're agreeable, I'd like you to use it to build a room on the back of the house for me. It'll keep me out from under foot, and give us all some privacy. The sooner you move me out of the parlor, the better." She opened the box to reveal dozens of gold and silver coins.

Angus stared at the money, then lifted his gaze to meet that of the old woman standing beside him.

After an awkward moment, she dumped the coins out on the table. "Go on, count it. I believe you'll find enough there to pay the cost." She had just sat down again when footsteps sounded on the stairs.

Toby nearly flew into the dining room. "Good morning, Grandma!" She returned the greeting, but he barely noticed, his attention suddenly riveted on the coins his father was stacking on the table. "We're rich!" he shouted gleefully, hurrying to his father's side to reach for a stack of coins.

Angus pushed Toby's hand away. "Don't touch, son. I'm counting."

His mother said, "The money isn't ours, Toby. It belongs to your grandmother, and she has asked your father to spend it to add a room to the house where she can live."

To his grandmother, Toby said, "Is it true, Grandma? Have you come to stay with us forever?"

His grandmother replied, "Not forever, Toby, but for the rest of my days, if your folks will have me."

"Mama, Papa, is Grandma going to live with us now?"

Mary remained silent, looking to Angus for a reply.

He paused in his counting to focus on Toby. "Yes, son. Your grandmother will be living with us for the rest of her days." He smiled tentatively at his mother-in-law, then resumed counting. When he had finished, he said, "There's more than enough here for an addition, and a parlor stove to keep it warm. With the company furnace shut down for replacement of the hearth, I can start today to hire a carpenter, and decide on the dimensions for the new room. And

I'll place an order for a new stove."

Toby cheered the pronouncement, adding, "I'm glad you're here to stay, Grandma!"

Flora came bursting into the room, immediately running to hug her grandmother. "Is it true, Grandma? Are you going to live with us, now?"

Grandma kissed her forehead. "It's true, child. I'm part of this family now."

"Oh, goody! Will you bake me some sugar cookies?"

"Of course, child. Of course," her grandmother promised with a hug. "Now you and your brother sit down to the table and I'll cook some eggs and bacon for your breakfast."

When she was gone, Mary said, "I'll have to suspend tutoring sessions once the construction is underway. The noise and confusion will be too much for the children to concentrate on school work."

Angus scowled. "I suppose you're right, but it seems a shame when you've barely made a start these last two weeks."

Lavinia said, "The children have just settled into the routine, coming here every day. They'll probably forget everything they've learned by the time the room is finished!"

Mary shrugged. "I don't know what else I can do."

Flora said, "You mean I won't get to see Alice and Grace every day?"

Toby said, "No, silly. It just means that they won't be coming *here*. We can go visit our friends at the shanties, can't we, Mama?"

"We'll see, Toby."

Angus tossed the coins into the tin box, then set his gaze on Mary. "Don't suspend the tutoring sessions just yet. I have an idea. Give me today to work things out." Stashing the coin box in the corner cabinet, he kissed Mary good bye and headed out the front door.

To Lavinia, the day seemed to pass on wings. Grandma, when she learned of the tutoring sessions for the immigrant children, insisted that she be allowed to take charge of all the cooking in order to free Mary and Lavinia for teaching responsibilities. The scholars arrived for their morning session at the usual time, and returned promptly after the midday meal for the afternoon. While lessons were underway, Angus brought a carpenter around to the back of the house to make measurements and mark the dimensions of the new room with wooden stakes and string. He took great care not to disturb the scholars until a few minutes before their dismissal. Entering the dining room, he stood at the head of the table and begged the attention of all.

"I have an important and exciting announcement to make!" He gazed about the room, taking in the immigrant scholars, his wife, and children. "Due to construction that will commence at the back of this house tomorrow, you will no longer report here for your lessons." Pausing to smile at Mary, he continued. "Tomorrow morning, you will report to the white house for your studies!"

"The Harris's?" Mary asked in disbelief.

The whispered words, "white house," passed among the children.

Angus continued. "Superintendent Harris and his wife have graciously offered the temporary use of their dining room until construction here is completed. You will be welcomed there at the regular time, and Mr. Harris's son, George, will join your class."

"Hooray!" Toby shouted.

"Hooray!" Chimed his classmates.

Chapter

7

On the following morning Lavinia and her mother, brother, and sister arrived at the Harris's with slates, slate pencils, reader, and arithmetic book in tow. Mrs. Harris greeted them cheerfully and led them immediately to the dining table where George sat ready with his own slate and school books.

Mrs. Harris pulled out the medallion-back chair that stood at the head of the oval cherry table and invited Mary to sit. "I trust you'll have enough room here to carry on your tutoring." To George, she said, "Son, you pay attention to Mrs. McAdams and learn the lessons she assigns. You'll not be allowed to join your father at the furnace until you've completed your recitations properly."

"Yes, ma'am," George replied, inviting Toby to sit in the chair next to his.

Lavinia gazed in awe around the impeccably decorated room with its chairs covered in burgundy velvet, its walls covered in wallpaper of dark red, blue, and creamy white berries against a white background, and its windows graced by navy blue velvet draperies. On the floor beneath her feet lay an especially thick, woolen carpet that incorporated all of those colors and more into a Chinese floral pattern. She couldn't help wondering whether such finery would stand up to the constant use of young children. The china cabinet at the end of the room displayed exquisite plates and bowls of delicate floral designs and much gilt, and crystal stemmed goblets within reach of small hands. The sterling silver service adorning the sideboard enticed inspection, too. She prayed that none of Mrs. Harris's breakables would fall to a shattering demise, and that her silver would be as tarnish- and dent-free on the last day as the first.

As the immigrant children arrived—many of them shoe-less on this warm spring day—she saw in them a special attentiveness to her mother's warnings to refrain from touching anything not their own. After a few minutes of gazing at the beauty surrounding them, they focused well on their schoolwork. George proved such a quick study that he completed his day's assignments including perfect recita-tion by midday, thus gaining his mother's permission to spend the afternoon with his father at the furnace where the replacement of the hearth was underway.

At home, Grandma had the midday meal ready and waiting, and immediately ladled up chicken soup thick with noodles. For dessert, she passed around a plate of soft, fat sugar cookies still warm from the oven that made Flora squeal with delight. When the hour-long dinner break was nearly over, Lavinia went out back with her father to see how the work on Grandma's new room was coming along. The area was being excavated to create a crawl space. Those who had been hired to do the job began returning from their dinner break. Lavinia was surprised to see Huck and Big Billy Bassett among them.

Huck approached her with a smile and tip of his cap. "Good afternoon, Lavinia!"

"Hello, Huck! I didn't know you and Billy were work-ing here," she admitted.

Her father explained. "They've been hired on to help out until the furnace goes into blast again."

Toby and Flora came out the back door, both greeting Huck in turn.

"Huck! Want to go fishing tonight?" Toby asked.

"Want to play your whistle for me so I can dance?" Flora asked, doing a quick heel-toe as he had taught her more than a month ago.

Huck offered a regretful smile and shook his head. "Sorry, Toby, Flora, not tonight. I have other plans."

Lavinia's heart plummeted, wondering with whom he could be planning to spend his evening.

Huck focused on Angus. "Sir, if you'll permit, I'd like to call on your elder daughter after supper this evening."

"I'll permit," Angus replied without hesitation. "The question is, will *she* permit." He turned to Lavinia. The smile that brightened her face outshone the sun.

Her face grew warm, and she knew it was not due to the heat of this fine May day. "I'll permit," she quietly agreed, then abruptly returned to the house to tell her mother and grandmother. She found them still sitting at the table, sipping tea. She sat again, words spilling from her mouth.

"Mama! Grandma! Huck just asked Papa if he could call on me tonight after supper!"

Her mother smiled approvingly.

Her grandmother said, "That Mr. Harrigan's a right fine fellow."

"How do you know?" Lavinia asked. "You only met him Sunday night."

"It's true," her grandmother admitted, "but he certainly conducted himself like a true gentleman, offering to bring me up to the Harris's. And this morning as I went about my chores in the kitchen, I could hear the fellows talking while they worked. Not a cuss word nor a complaint nor a disparaging remark passed his lips. I can't say the same for the others."

Mary said, "Mr. Harrigan does have an exceptionally civil tongue and pleasant disposition." She set her empty cup in its saucer and rose. "It's nearly time to resume class. Please call the children, Lavinia. We don't want to be late."

Lavinia could hardly keep her mind on the afternoon lessons at the Harris's. She kept thinking of Huck and his visit and wondering what they would do. They couldn't sit on the sofa and play parlor games with that room now converted to Grandma's bedroom. She shuddered at the thought that they may have to spend their evening in conversation at the dining table. It may be a convenient place to set their teacups and cookies, but they would have no privacy at all if the younger children joined them, which undoubtedly they would. As the afternoon wore on she grew fretful. Certain that the evening would be a disaster, she wondered why she had agreed to his visit in the first place. Her mood plummeted further when, on the walk home from the Harris's, Toby and Flora followed her singing a chant.

"Livvy's sweet on Huck! Livvy's sweet on Huck!"

She spun around. "Hush, you two! I am *not!*"

"Are too!" they argued in unison.

"Am *not!*"

Toby said, "If you're not sweet on Huck, then why did you say he could come calling?"

Flora chimed in. "Yes, why, Livvy?"

She looked for their mother to intervene, but she was several yards behind, talking with some of the other students. Suddenly, a tart reply flew off Lavinia's tongue. "I agreed to see Huck tonight so he wouldn't have to spend the evening fishing or playing his whistle with you children!" A crestfallen look overspread each of their faces, but

Lavinia didn't care. She only wanted to be free of their taunts. Setting a rapid pace, she hurried home and dashed up the stairs, closing the bedroom door and turning the key. Not a minute later, Flora tried to enter, then began pounding on the locked door.

"Let me in!"

"Go away! I thought you were going to O'Connells' to nurse Cubby."

"Not today. Grandma said she'd help me mend Tilly." Flora referred to the rag doll on her bed. "I've come to get her. Now let me in!"

Angrily, Lavinia fetched the doll, opened the door, and shoved it at Flora. "Here! Now, leave me alone!" Slamming the door and locking it again, she returned to her bed. Moments later she heard another knock followed by her mother's firm request. "Lavinia, unlock your door, please."

Reluctantly, Lavinia obeyed, then flopped onto her bed, face buried in her pillow.

Her mother closed the door, then sat on the bed beside her, stroking her hair. "What's the matter, dear?"

Lavinia mumbled her reply. "Sometimes I wish I were an only child."

"Now, what would make you feel that way?" Mary gently prodded.

Lavinia sat up and told of the words that had been exchanged amongst herself, Toby, and Flora on the way home, including her own terse reply to their teasing. "I wish Huck weren't even coming here tonight," she continued. "The children are going to make the evening miserable!"

Mary lay a comforting arm about Lavinia's shoulders. "I know it's hard to stand the teasing when a fellow takes a liking to you, and you to him. I'll have a talk with Toby and Flora, but I'd like you to talk to them, too, and tell them you're sorry for what you said. Will you do that, please?"

Lavinia's gaze was downcast. After a moment's thought, she quietly mumbled, "Yes, Mama."

Her mother lifted her chin, kissed her on the cheek, and then smiled. "Now, I have an idea for an outing tonight when Huck comes to call. How would you like it if you and Huck and your father and I all took a walk while Grandma watches over Toby and Flora? I'll make sure your father and I don't follow you and Huck too close."

Lavinia smiled. "Do you mean it, Mama?"

"Of course I mean it! Now come downstairs. You need to have that talk with your brother and sister, then your grandmother could use our help setting the table and getting supper on."

When all were seated for supper, the blessing said, and thick ham sandwiches passed around, Angus pulled an envelope from his pocket. "I received a letter from Big Toby's kin today."

Lavinia quickly asked, "Are his folks coming for him?"

Angus shook his head. Opening the letter, he began to read. "'Dear Mr. McAdams: The lost boy you described fits the description of my nephew, Chauncey Chandler. He took sick last summer from heat stroke. Since then, he has not been right in the head. He has no mama or papa. For the last year he has been living with me, his spinster aunt. No other kin would take him in.

"'This spring he wandered off. I am not fit to travel to Fayette, my legs being crippled from arthritis, nor do I have the money to come even if my legs was good. He got there by his own power, and if he wishes to return to me, he will have to come back the same way. Sorry I cannot do more.

"'Yours truly, Miss Edna Chandler, Marquette, Michigan.'"

Angus folded the letter and returned it to his pocket. "I stopped by the hotel and read the letter to Big Toby before I came home. He grew very anxious at the suggestion of returning to Marquette and begged Mr. Rose to keep him on. Mr. Rose said he would be pleased to keep Big Toby as his hire so long as he continues to work hard the way he has these last two weeks. Tomorrow I will write to Miss Chandler and inform her of her nephew's status."

Lavinia said, "Thank goodness all is working out so well for Big Toby—Chauncey rather."

Little Toby said, "And thank goodness we can start calling him by his rightful name. I'm mighty tired of having to lend him *my* name."

Angus said, "Son, I'm afraid you're just going to have to get used to it. When I called Big Toby 'Chauncey', he grew agitated and adamantly insisted that everybody continue calling him by his new name."

Mary said, "I can't help wondering what happened up in Marquette that would make him run away and change his name."

Flora said, "Maybe his Aunt Edna was mean and cruel."

Toby said, "Maybe he stole something—like candy or cookies or tarts—and was about to get caught, so he ran away and took on a new name."

Grandma said, "Now, children, we'd best not speculate about the wrongdoing of others when the truth is not at hand. I found Big Toby to be a pleasant fellow the night I arrived, even if he is a bit touched in the head. And as for his Aunt Edna, she was kind enough to take him in when no one else would have him."

Lavinia said, "Grandma's right. We simply have to accept Big Toby for what we know is true."

Conversation turned to the progress on Grandma's new room and plans for the evening. Lavinia was especially pleased to hear her mother's explicit instructions to Toby and Flora to obey their grandmother and help with the washing up after supper.

Her mother continued. "Your father, sister, and I are going for a walk, and while we're gone, I want the two of you to be on your best behavior. Do you understand?"

"Yes, Mama," they answered with disappointment.

Then Flora asked, "Mama, may Toby and I take Grandma to see Cubby after we finish the dishes?"

"If your grandmother wishes to go, you have my permission."

"Thank you, Mama!" She immediately began telling her grandmother about the fox cub she and Toby had found in the woods, convincing her to go and see the little creature.

After the cookies had been served, Lavinia went up to her room to comb her hair and wash her face in preparation for Huck's arrival. As she fussed with her hair, making certain that it lay neatly against her shoulders, she smiled at the thought that she would be nearly alone with Huck for the entire evening. At least their conversation would be private, as her mother had promised. Even the weather had cooperated on this fine spring evening, sending a warm but gentle breeze through her open window to caress her cheek and surround her with the earthly aroma of the reawakening woodlands. Satisfied with her appearance, she looked out the window in the direction of town. The sight of Huck coming up the lane at a brisk pace caused her heart to skip a beat. She hurried downstairs to tell her mother and to wait for his knock. Determined not to appear eager, she waited for his second knock before answering.

The moment Huck saw Lavinia, the words he had been rehearsing on the walk from the hotel flew from his mind. Instead, he could think only of the loveliness of her smile, the attractiveness of her dark brown hair against the true blue of her dress, and the sparkle that put an irresistible light in her brown eyes.

Lavinia thought Huck had never looked more handsome than he did at this very instant, with his fiery hair neatly parted and combed so that it fell gently against his forehead. His shirt lay open at the collar exposing his strong, thick neck, and his mouth hinted at a smile that was about to materialize.

Although reluctant to spoil the magic of the moment, Lavinia realized that she needed to explain the plan for the evening. Her words tumbled out.

"Mama has suggested that you and I, and she and Papa all take a walk this evening—that is, if you don't mind. You see, if we stay here, we'll have to sit in the dining room, because the parlor is now Grandma's bedroom. So it would be best if we all take a walk together and enjoy the fine weather this evening, don't you think? Mama promises she and Papa won't follow us too close."

Huck barely knew how to respond. His own plans had changed since he'd asked permission to call on her, and his gift of blarney, so desperately needed at this very instant, had been blown clean away by Lavinia's rush of words. He offered a smile and a question. "Have you and your folks decided on a route for the evening walk?"

"A route?" Lavinia asked mindlessly, trying to decide on the most pleasant path. Bereft of ideas, she replied thoughtfully, "No, come to think of it, we haven't."

"Ah! Then may I suggest one?"

Lavinia nodded.

"Perhaps we could start by heading in the direction of the cabins by the beach."

Unimpressed, but unwilling to argue, Lavinia replied simply, "Perhaps."

Huck continued. "There's a very good reason for going that way, and I'd like to explain it to you and your folks, if I may?"

Lavinia's parents joined her and Huck in the entryway as if on cue. Mary greeted him cheerfully, then asked, "Did you say that you wished to explain something?"

Huck nodded. "I've come to extend an invitation to you and your family—Grandma, too—to a bonfire and an evening of old-fashioned, Irish storytelling. It's to be held on the beach over by the cabins. Big Billy and Paddy and I came upon the idea after we finished work here this afternoon. The fellows that live in the cabins are stacking the firewood this very minute. The O'Connells and the Reillys will be there along with their little ones, and I thought you all would enjoy it. I'd be especially pleased if Lavinia, Toby, and Flora could hear the stories I used to hear when I was growing up—the Finn-tales about the Irish heroes, and the story of how the Shannon got its name. And Paddy plans to tell a tale about a white trout that would be sure to tickle Toby's fancy."

Lavinia's heart sank. All afternoon she had been looking forward to enjoying the company of Huck alone, or almost alone, and now he wanted her to spend the evening with her brother and sister and a whole crowd of people! Quietly, she said, "Please excuse me."

Huck watched helplessly as she turned and fled up the stairs. He'd seen the sparkle going out of her eyes and the smile fading from her lips as he had been talking. To Angus and Mary he said, "I'm afraid I've said something wrong."

Mary said, "I'll go talk to her."

Lavinia flopped on her bed. Though tears began welling in her eyes, a knot of anger prevented her from sobbing. Her mother sat down beside her and gently caressed her shoulder. "What is it, dear? Don't you want to go to the bonfire?"

Lavinia shook her head, the knot in her throat tighter than ever. *Why did Huck have to go and spoil it all? Why couldn't they spend the evening the way she and her mother had planned?*

Mary continued. "Huck will be mighty disappointed, but I'll tell him you'd rather stay home alone, if that's what you wish."

Lavinia hated the thought of missing out. She hated it more than the thought of sharing Huck with everyone else for the evening. Hearing her mother's footsteps heading for the door, she quickly rose to her feet.

"Mama?"

"Yes, dear?"

"Tell Huck I'll be right down."

Her mother smiled. "I'll tell him, dear."

Lavinia washed all evidence of tears from her eyes and practiced putting on a smile again. Taking a deep breath, she prayed for grace and good humor, exhaled the last shreds of disappointment, and headed downstairs.

Huck, Toby, Flora, and Grandma were waiting for her in the entryway.

Grandma said, "Your mother and father have decided to stay home and take care of the washing up. If you're ready, dear, we'll be on our way."

"I'm ready, Grandma," she said with a smile.

Placing her hand on the arm Huck offered, they followed the others out the door and down the road to town.

Chapter 8

As Huck and Lavinia approached the beach at the shanty village, she could see that daylight was fast fading in the western sky, and a rosy red hue had eased upward from the horizon in a blaze of flaming glory that seemed to set the lake on fire. Voices of anticipation filled the air. Children called to one another with excitement while they searched for driftwood kindling. Chickens clucked, dogs barked, and a cow mooed in response to the commotion. Flora insisted on stopping by the O'Connell cabin to introduce Grandma to Cubby, even though no one but Shamrock and her brood were at home. Joining the others near the site of the bonfire, Lavinia and her grandmother sat on a log bench while Huck helped the fellows place the last of the heavy wood on the stack, and Toby and Flora sought their friends, the O'Connells and the Reillys.

Huck introduced Grandma to Moira and the O'Connells, Mr. and Mrs. Reilly, and the other families who occupied the beach cabins, then sat beside Lavinia, pressing close as others joined them on the log bench. With the grayness of dusk fading to the dark of night, Big Billy and Paddy lit the driftwood kindling. It sputtered, sparked, smoked, and crackled. Then tiny flames licked at the dry timber. Within minutes they grew into great tongues of fire, sending up a fragrant smoke that drifted out over the water on a mild offshore breeze.

In the flickering light of the bonfire, Paddy began to speak.

"I've a tale to tell of the white trout, and it's especially for Toby McAdams that I'm telling it." He paused to wink at the boy, whose gaze was riveted on him. "There was once upon a time, long ago, a beautiful lady who lived in a castle on a lake. She was promised to a king's son, but before they could be married, he was murdered and thrown into the lake.

"As the story goes, she went out of her mind with sorrow and the fairies took her away. Then in the course of time, a white trout appeared in the stream that flowed from the lake. No one knew what to think of the creature, for none like it had ever been seen before, but for years it swam there.

"The people began to think that it was a fairy, and no one dared harm it. Then one day a soldier came to fish in the stream and the people warned him not to take the white trout. But the blackguard laughed at them and caught the trout and took it home.

"He put the frying pan over his fire and pitched in the trout. At that very instant the trout squealed to high heavens." Paddy let out a blood-curdling scream that sent chills through Lavinia.

Alice and Grace O'Connell squealed with delight, then Alice eagerly asked, "What happened next, Da?"

Paddy put on a wicked smile. "The soldier only laughed. He cooked the trout and cooked it some more and turned it and turned it, but the fish showed no sign of the fire. Finally, he said, 'Maybe you taste better than you look,' and he cut into it.

"Then came a murderous screech even louder than before that 'd scare the life out of you if ever you heard it.

Instantly the trout jumped out of the pan into the middle of the floor and rose up as a beautiful lady, the most beautiful creature the soldier had ever seen!" To Grace, Paddy said, "And what do you suppose she was wearing?"

"She wore a dress of white and a band of gold in her hair!" Grace answered.

"That's right!" Paddy exclaimed.

Before he could continue, Alice added, "And a stream of blood ran down her arm!"

"So it did!" Paddy confirmed. "And the lady said to the soldier, 'Look where you cut me! Why didn't you leave me in the stream?'

"The soldier shook with fear until his boots rattled. He begged her forgiveness and pleaded for his life.

"Then she said to him, 'I was on duty in the stream, watching for my true love who will come by water to me, and if he comes while I am away, I'll turn you into a snake!'

"Again, the soldier begged for mercy and she said to him, 'Repent your evil ways and be a good man from now on. You can start by putting me back in the river where you found me.'

"The soldier opened his mouth to argue but before he could get out the first word, she turned into a fish again. So he put her onto a clean plate and ran as fast as he could to the river. The moment she hit the water, it turned red as blood. Then the stain washed away and to this day there's a little red mark on the trout's side.

"And from that time on the soldier never ate fish, and he reformed his ways and prayed every day for the soul of the white trout."

Toby said, "I never heard of a white trout till now. I don't think there's any such thing!"

Paddy chuckled. "Perhaps you're right. But if you should ever, by chance, hook into a creature like I described, you be sure to put it right back, or you might turn into a snake!"

Everyone laughed, then the children begged Paddy to tell them more.

He said, "Now, I'll tell you about Finn's people, the legendary warriors."

Flora spoke up. "Who was Finn?"

Paddy smiled. "Finn MacCool was a great man who lived in the third century. He was the son of Cumal, Chief of the Fian of Munster and Leinster in the east and south of Ireland."

Huck leaned close to Lavinia. Slipping his arm about her, he said quietly, "This was one of my favorite stories when I was a boy."

Lavinia tried to focus on Paddy's words, but for a few moments, all she could think of was the wondrous warmth of Huck's hand resting gently on her waist, and the satisfying sense of security that now enfolded her. Content in his embrace, she turned her attention to Paddy once more, learning that any one of Finn's people could recite twelve books of poetry. He could defend himself against nine other warriors without being injured; run through the woods without breaking a branch; jump over a stick set at brow's height without touching it; and pass under one set at knee's height without touching it.

When Paddy had finished, Toby spoke up. "That's impossible, Mr. O'Connell! Nobody could do all that!"

Paddy smiled. "My lad, you're right! A mere man could never pass the test. But when we slip back for a time into the magical mists of ancient Erin, anything is possible! Hear now, Huck's story of Finn's son, Oisin."

Huck withdrew his arm from Lavinia and rested it on his thigh as he spoke. The absence of his touch made her feel strangely cold and alone even though the bonfire still sent its warmth into the night air, and he was still close beside her. But as he began to tell of Oisin, the brave and gentle hero poet, and Niamh of the Golden Hair from the far off country of Tir na nOg, Lavinia lost herself in the story.

She imagined that she was the princess on the white horse, robes flowing, heart set on the noble Oisin of whom she had heard tell. And she saw, too, the perfect blend of virility and tenderness in Oisin when he pledged his love to her. To the Land of Virtues they sped, where Niamh's beloved Oisin fought the giant, Fomor of the Blows, before arriving with her safely in the Land of Youth. There, a great banquet was held for ten days and ten nights, and on the final day, Niamh was given in marriage to her sweetheart.

Lavinia imagined the pleasant amusements and feasting in the Land of Youth where beauty and strength never faded, and where three hundred years passed as quickly as three years. When Oisin grew eager to visit his father in Ireland again, she could envision Niamh giving him her white steed, and warning him that if he should set his foot on the sod of Erin, he could never return to her.

Huck continued. "Oisin was greatly sorrowed to find his father's castle tumbled down and overgrown with weeds. He rode on, coming shortly to a number of men try-ing to raise a large, flat stone. Those under it were not strong enough to raise it farther and were on the point of being crushed when they begged for Oisin's help.

"He leaned forward and seized the rock with one hand, flinging it to the far end of the field, but the strain broke the golden saddle-girth. Though he struggled to keep from falling, he slid off the white steed, coming to his feet on the sod of Erin. The horse ran off, fast as the wind. And just as quickly, a change came over Oisin. His sight, beauty, and strength left him and he fell to the soil a withered, wrinkled, and feeble man, never to see his beloved Niamh of the Golden Hair again."

Huck's gaze met Lavinia's, inviting her reaction.

"That's a sad tale," she said quietly.

He nodded, reaching for her hand.

While the storytelling continued with Moira spinning the tale of St. Brigid's Cloak, Lavinia sat in perfect contentment, her hand enfolded in Huck's large, warm ones. Though she tried to focus on what Moira was saying, her thoughts kept slipping back to the tale Huck had told. In her mind, she pictured Oisin remaining on his steed and fighting many battles on his return trip, finally reunited with Niamh to live happily ever after in the Land of Youth where their children were born and raised.

Moira continued with the stories of the Giant's Stair and the Crookened Back. By the time she had finished, the youngest children had fallen asleep in their mothers' laps, and Toby and Flora were beginning to yawn.

Grandma said, "The hour is late. We'd best get on home."

Huck lit a torch, then he and Lavinia led Grandma and the children along the path. They hadn't gone far when Huck said, "The air is cool and damp away from the fire, don't you think?"

"It is," Lavinia replied, the chill penetrating her cotton dress.

Huck slipped his arm about her and drew her close, sending his warmth through her and making her wish they had miles to walk rather than just the short hike up the road.

As they approached the front door, Grandma said, "I'm

going to brew some tea. You're welcome to join us, Huck."

He shook his head. "Thanks, anyway. I'll be taking my leave as soon as I've said good night to Lavinia."

Grandma nodded, then ushered the younger children inside and stood by the open door staring at Huck and Lavinia.

Lavinia grew immediately uncomfortable and was about to go inside when her mother came to the front door and addressed Grandma firmly.

"Close the door, if you please. There's a cold draft running through the house."

"What?" Grandma replied indignantly. "And leave these two young folks out here alone in the dark?"

"You needn't worry. You said yourself that Huck is a true gentleman," Mary reminded her.

"Maybe so," the old woman admitted, " but in my day, a girl's reputation could be ruined in circumstances such as this."

Huck slipped his arm from Lavinia's waist. "I'd best be going."

Mary said, "You'll stay right there, young man, until you've bid Lavinia good night." To Grandma she said, "It's time we go and brew some tea."

"But—"

"*Now*, Mother," Mary insisted. To Lavinia, she said, "You have three minutes to say good night to Huck. If you're not in the house by then, your grandmother will come get you."

"Yes, Mama," Lavinia replied, thankful when the front door closed, leaving her alone with Huck, if only for a short while.

He planted his torch in the ground, then took both of Lavinia's hands in his. All concern for time fled as he gazed into her face, finding there a beauty that would have put Niamh to shame. He studied Lavinia's lips, curved in a tentative smile, and wanted nothing more than to taste their honey, but he restrained himself, resorting to a few simple words instead.

"Thank you for coming tonight."

So close was his mouth that Lavinia could feel the warmth of his breath when he spoke. She thought of how silly she had been earlier to ever consider staying home and missing out on this magical evening.

"Thank you for inviting me," she replied, studying the lines of his cheek and jaw and finding them to be more handsome than even the comely Oisin of her mind.

Desire rising within him and time running short, Huck swiftly released Lavinia's hands, grabbed his torch, and backed away. "Good night! I'll see you tomorrow!"

"Good night!" she replied, feeling too suddenly abandoned as she watched the flame of his torch disappearing in the direction of the hotel. Letting herself in, she answered her mother's question of how the evening had gone with a minimum of words and headed straight up to bed to relive the last few hours all over again in her dreams.

Morning came too soon, and despite the aroma of coffee and bacon, and the thick, golden flapjack that Grandma flipped onto her plate, Lavinia's appetite couldn't be stirred. By the time the others had eaten two pancakes apiece, she had finished only a few bites.

Her mother addressed her with concern. "Lavinia, are you feeling all right?"

"Fine, Mama," she answered absently, her mind still on Huck.

Grandma said, "You'd better eat up, girl, or you'll be hungry halfway through your morning lessons."

"Yes, Grandma," Lavinia replied, setting her fork to the task with more purpose. But the images of Huck lingered, along with the new and wonderful sensation that seemed to put her in another world.

Six weeks later—end of June

As Lavinia spread the frosting on the maple cake her mother had baked for Flora's birthday, she was thankful that school was now in recess until September. The warm weather had made scholars eager to be at play outdoors, just as Flora and her two best friends, the O'Connell twins, were right now. She could hear their happy voices in the back yard, interspersed with the hammers at work in Grandma's soon-to-be-finished room. Over the last several weeks many secret plans had been undertaken to make it a special, homey place. Many times, her father and brother had abandoned unfruitful fishing outings and devoted their time instead to their special woodworking projects at the carpenters' shed near the furnace. Their lack of fish had become somewhat of a joke with Grandma, who couldn't understand how they could catch so little when they were so often seen leaving the house with poles and net.

The resulting progress on Grandma's room had greatly pleased Lavinia's folks, but progress of a different sort had pleased Lavinia the most—that of her friendship with Huck. Since the night of Irish storytelling, he had come to call every evening. Sometimes, he would take her to the carpenters' shed where he would work alongside her father and brother. While the men put their hands to planers and sanders, saws and chisels, she would sit quietly on a stool and put needle and thread to work on a secret sewing project for Grandma that she had smuggled out of the house beneath her skirt.

With Huck's evening visits, and Grandma in Fayette to stay, time seemed to pass on winged feet, rather than the ironclad ones that had made days drag by when Lavinia had first come to this town. She hardly ever thought about the eighth of August anymore, and her plan to return to Canada. Huck was ever on her mind, and today, he was coming for the midday meal to help celebrate Flora's seventh birthday.

The shrill peal of the furnace whistle signaled that Huck and her father would be here in a few minutes. Lavinia smoothed the last of the frosting over the cake, then arranged maple sugar candies on top as decorations.

Her mother paused to admire the confection, then handed Lavinia a candle. "I do believe this is the prettiest cake Flora has ever had. It's almost a shame to ruin it with a candle."

Lavinia pressed the five-inch stub of a taper candle deep into the very center. "Flora would be terribly disappointed if she didn't have a candle to blow out on her birthday."

Grandma voiced her agreement, then opened the oven and removed a large casserole dish covered with a golden brown crust. "Flora won't be disappointed in the chicken pie she requested for her birthday dinner. It's done to perfection." She set it on the table then turned to Lavinia. "Your sister's present is hidden away in my trunk—the one near the window. It's wrapped in brown paper and tied with pink satin ribbon. You'll fetch it when the time comes, won't you, Lavinia?"

"Of course!" she replied, envisioning her little sister's reaction to the fancy gift that she and her mother had helped her grandmother to complete over the past few weeks. She was eager, too, to see the gift her father, brother, and Huck were giving Flora. She had seen it partly finished at the carpenters' shed, but it was a well-kept secret as to exactly what it would look like when completed.

Within minutes everyone had gathered at the dining table and Angus asked a blessing.

"We thank thee, Lord, for this special day in the life of our little Flora, and the dear friends who have gathered with us to celebrate her seventh birthday. Bless this food to our use, in Jesus name, Amen." Picking up a large serving spoon, he broke the crust of the chicken pie and spooned a portion onto a warm plate. "The first piece is for our birthday girl!" He passed it to her, then served the others.

After a few bites, Flora said, "I can hardly wait to see my birthday presents!"

Toby said, "Maybe we won't give you any!"

Angus said, "Don't be mean, son. You know she'll get something very nice."

Alice O'Connell said, "Nicer than the birthday spanking Mama and Papa always give Grace and me, I expect."

Huck said, "You're right! And nicer than the birthday bumps I always got when I was little."

Flora's brow wrinkled. "Birthday bumps?"

Huck nodded. "When I was small, Papa would pick me up by the ankles and bump my head on the floor once for every year of my age, plus one for good measure."

Mary chuckled. "Now I know how he knocked so much good sense into your head."

Grandma said, "When I was a little girl in Scotland, my birthday celebrations were quite different from this one. I remember the year I turned seven . . ." She told about the riddle she had to solve in order to find her one and only birthday gift, a peppermint stick.

When she had finished, Angus and Mary each described their favorite birthdays. By the time they had finished, the chicken potpie had been consumed and Lavinia and her mother and grandmother cleared the table and lit the candle on Flora's cake. Lavinia carried it to the table, being careful not to let the flame go out, and set it in front of Flora, saying, "Now make a wish and blow out the candle."

Flora squeezed her eyes shut, then opened them wide, took a deep breath, and blew out the flame.

Alice and Grace applauded, saying almost in unison, "Your wish will come true!"

Toby asked, "What did you wish for?"

Flora said, "I wished that whoever finds the blessing coin will give it to me."

Toby said, "If *I* find it, I'm giving it to Huck!"

Huck asked, "What is a blessing coin?"

Angus said, "You may have heard of lucky cakes."

Huck nodded, remembering the tradition in his cousins' family of baking a coin into the birthday cake and believing that whoever found it would become rich.

Angus continued. "In our family, we don't believe in luck, but we *do* believe in blessings. Whenever someone has a birthday, Mary bakes a blessing coin into the cake. Whoever finds the coin is twice blessed, first by receiving it, and then by giving it away. And of course, the one who ends up with the coin is blessed, too."

Lavinia cut the cake into nine pieces and passed them around. Moments later, Huck held up a copper penny.

"I've been blessed!" He declared.

Toby said, "Now, bless *me*, Huck!"

Flora said, "No, *me!*"

Huck smiled. "Maybe I'll give it to Alice or Grace." He smiled at the twins, then shifted his gaze to Lavinia. "Or maybe I should give it to your sister." After a moment's thought, he told Flora, "But I will give it to the birthday girl."

Flora beamed. "Thank you, Huck! I just knew you would!"

Mary said, "Go upstairs right now and put it in your piggy bank so you won't lose it."

Flora scowled. "But I was going to spend it on candy at the store."

Mary shook her head. "You've already had candy on the top of your birthday cake, remember? Now, do as I say, and when you come back, you may have your birthday gifts."

"Yes, Mama," Flora replied, then hurried up the stairs.

Chapter

9

While Flora was upstairs putting the blessing coin in her piggy bank, Lavinia retrieved the brown paper package from Grandma's trunk and set it on her sister's chair. When Flora returned, Mary told her, "This gift is from Grandma, Lavinia, and me."

Flora wasted no time untying the pink satin ribbon and folding back the brown paper. When she saw the fancily clad cloth doll, she gasped with delight. "This is the most beautiful dolly I've ever seen!"

Lavinia watched with satisfaction as her sister gently ran her fingers over the dress Grandma had made—the pink smocked bodice, the flounced silk skirt, and the row of tiny hearts embroidered above the lace-edged hem. Below it, the shoes Lavinia had sewn of black fabric and buttoned into place caught Flora's attention. Then she ran her hand over the sandy-colored yarn braids her mother had fashioned and stitched into place to imitate her own. They were tied at the ends with pink satin ribbon matching the dress—the same shade as the blush Lavinia had embroidered on the doll's cheeks. Flora traced the mouth embroidered in red silk floss and the blue eyes and blond brows, then hugged the doll tightly to her chest, uttering, "Thank you Mama, Grandma, Lavinia. I'll keep this dolly forever!"

Angus said, "Now that you have your new doll, Toby will fetch the gift that he and Huck and I made."

Toby ran out back and returned moments later carrying

a large object draped in cloth. He set it on the floor beside his younger sister. "Happy Birthday, Flora!"

Instantly, she snatched off the drape, revealing a doll-size wooden rocking chair.

Everyone gathered around, and Lavinia noticed immediately that this was no ordinary doll's rocker. The head-piece had been finely chiseled with illustrations of nursery rhymes. On the left was a pie of blackbirds, and on the right, an old woman in a shoe. They bordered the plain oval in the center, to which Toby pointed, telling Flora, "When you think of a name for your doll, Huck will put it right here, between the pictures he carved. Papa cut out all the pieces for the chair and put them together, and I did all the sanding. It took us a whole month to finish!"

Flora put her doll on the chair—a perfect fit—then rocked it back and forth, her eyes gleaming. "Thank you Toby, Papa, Huck! This chair and doll are the best birthday presents ever!"

Angus smiled. "I'm glad you like them, Flora." The words were barely out of his mouth when the whistle blew signaling the end of the dinner hour. "Huck and I have to get back to work. I'll see you at suppertime. Enjoy your day, Flora!"

"I will, Papa. I will!"

Lavinia ran her fingers over the images on the head-piece of the rocker, and the smooth finish of its arms. "This is quite a keepsake, Flora. You must take very good care of this chair."

Grandma nodded, adding, "And you must take good care of your new doll, too."

Mary said, "She's an indoor doll. You are not to play with her outside. You will soil her dress, and then it will be ruined. It's not cotton like your old dolly's dress that can be easily washed."

"Yes, Mama," Flora replied. "May Alice and Grace and I play with my new doll upstairs?"

"You may. Toby will carry her chair up for you."

When the children had gone, Grandma began stacking dirty dishes, saying, "I've never seen a chair the likes of that one. With Huck's talent, I should think he could get work in some cabinetmaker's shop as a wood carver."

As Lavinia helped carry the dishes to the kitchen, the words lingered in her mind. Perhaps his experience in the carpenter's shop in Wisconsin had turned out poorly, but it seemed a shame that his talent for woodcarving should go to waste while he performed the heavy labor of a pig iron man.

Late that night, after Huck had called on Lavinia and returned to his quarters at the hotel, he took pen in hand and wrote a letter to his Uncle Sean. A month ago, when he had been seeing Lavinia steadily for three weeks, he had told briefly of their friendship. Now, he expanded his description of her kin, giving an account of the gift he had helped make for Flora and the wonderful birthday dinner he had shared with the McAdams family.

> *. . . Enclosed is another draft. God willing, I will have repaid you the entire cost of my passage by year's end. I thank you for sending me here, Uncle Sean. Though the work be tiring and dirty, the rewards are great. I have never been happier in my life! Your nephew, Huck*

Ten days later—second week of July

Lavinia hummed as she helped her mother set the supper table, for tonight, after two months of disruptions on the first floor of the house, a special meal had been planned to celebrate the completion of the new room. For the last week while the finishing work was underway, Grandma had been forbidden to enter on the promise that a very special surprise was in store. Today, Lavinia and her mother had worked especially hard to move Grandma's belongings from the parlor to the new room and put every last detail in place. The very thought of the wonderful sight that would soon meet Grandma's eyes gave Lavinia's heart a lift.

She hummed, too, because Huck would be joining them for the meal, and afterward, they would sit in the parlor where they could enjoy a greater measure of privacy, rather than at the dining table where Toby and Flora constantly interrupted their conversations.

Sometimes she found it difficult to believe that Flora was seven years old, and that yesterday, Toby had reached a full twelve years. Their methods of gaining Huck's attention had at times seemed like the antics of five-year-olds. Now that Grandma's new room would be a haven for the youngsters as she herself had requested, they would have no excuse to linger in the parlor.

Lavinia hoped and prayed that the added space would ease the tension between her mother and grandmother, too, but she supposed that was too much to expect. Even though her grandmother was in charge of all the cooking, her mother seemed at loose ends with no scholars to tutor, and when she tried to help in the kitchen, the bickering would start.

The furnace whistle blew, signaling suppertime. Lavinia finished setting the table, then helped her grandmother to spread the filling on the wild blueberry cake she had baked especially for tonight. Huck and her father arrived home and washed up, then her mother called everyone to the table.

Angus asked a blessing. "Thank you, Lord for good food to bring an end to a good day. Thank you that Grandma can sleep in her own room tonight. Thank you that the furnace is doing better than ever since the new hearth was put in last May. And thank you for the new man I hired today, so strong he can do the work of two men. Now bless this food to our use, in Jesus' name, Amen." He helped himself to the meat, then passed the platter along, saying, "The fellow I hired today could probably finish off every piece of this ham all by himself, don't you think, Huck?"

He nodded. "That fellow must weigh at least three hundred pounds!"

Mary asked, "Where is he from?"

Angus replied, "Out East, Pennsylvania. He came to me claiming he could wheel a ton of pigs to the dock all by himself. I told him I'd give him a try, so when we ran out the iron, he loaded up a wheelbarrow with twenty pigs. And by goodness, he moved it to the dock without a single bit of help!"

Grandma asked, "What's this fellow's name? Samson?"

Angus chuckled. "No, his name is Arthur Walters. His arm is thicker than my thigh, and his waist is twice my girth."

Mary said, "Thank goodness he's not eating at our table tonight. He might decide to finish off Grandma's cake all by himself, and who would argue?"

Toby spoke up. "I would!"

Flora echoed, "I would!"

Lavinia said, "Then Papa would send you both upstairs without dessert for arguing at the table!"

Laughter filled the room. But the happy sound was suddenly interrupted when the front door banged open and Big Toby burst into the room, his face pale as limestone.

"He's come to get me! He's gonna kill me! You got to help me! *Please!*"

Angus and Huck both sprang to Big Toby's side, Angus saying, "Calm down, son. Nobody wants to kill you!" He placed a reassuring arm about the boy's shoulder, but Big Toby pulled away, shuffling agitatedly.

"You're wrong! He's gonna kill me! He said so!"

"*Who* said so?" Angus asked.

"A big, huge man! He came to town today! Now he's gonna kill me just like he said! Don't let him kill me, Mr. McAdams! *Please!*" He crumpled to the floor, face in hands, asking through his sobs, "What am I gonna do? *What am I gonna do?*"

Angus bent down, taking hold of the boy's elbow. "Come into the parlor with us, son. You'll be safe there."

Big Toby peeked out through his fingers at Angus and Huck. "Are you sure?"

Angus nodded. "We're sure."

"Really sure?"

Huck said, "Absolutely, positively sure!"

Reluctantly, the boy rose to his feet. Angus and Huck escorted him across the hall to the parlor.

From the dining room, Lavinia could faintly hear her father telling Big Toby, "Now start at the beginning and tell me all about this big man who wants to kill you."

Curious to hear his explanation, Lavinia excused herself to take Big Toby a glass of cold water. He accepted it thankfully, drank a few sips, and continued his story. Lavinia sat down to listen.

"Like I said, I saw him walking down the street in

Marquette one night."

Angus asked, "When was that? Do you remember?"

Big Toby nodded. "A couple of weeks before I met you."

Huck said, "So that would have been about the second week of April."

"I guess so," Big Toby replied.

Angus said, "So this big fellow was walking down the street, and then what?"

"He came to the saloon and stopped. I thought he was gonna go inside, but he turned away. Just then, a fellow came out of the saloon, stumbled down the step, and slammed into the big man. He didn't mean to do it, he just lost his balance!" Big Toby paused, a pained expression on his face and a faraway look in his eyes.

Angus said, "Go on, son. A fellow slammed into the big man, and what did the big man do?"

Big Toby focused on Angus again. "The big man pushed him. Then the other fellow got real angry. He called the big man a bad name and was gonna hit him." The boy leaped from his chair and swung his arm in a circle as if winding up for a punch. "But before he could do it, the big fellow cracked him in the jaw." He put his hand to his left cheek and staggered back, landing on the sofa. "When the smaller fellow went down, he hit his head on the step and didn't get up."

Huck said, "So the smaller man was unconscious."

Big Toby shook his head vehemently. "He was dead!"

Lavinia said, "How did you know that?"

"The big fellow grabbed him by the shoulders and shook him and shook him. When he didn't come to, the big fellow left him right there and turned to run away. That's when he saw me watching. He came up to me and grabbed me by the shirt and told me that if I said one word, the same thing would happen to me. Then he let me go with such a push I fell on my backside. I was so scared I just sat there looking up at him. Then he said, 'Go on, git!' So I scrambled to my feet and I ran, and I ran, and finally I ended up at Mr. Rose's hotel!" He paused to take another sip of water.

Angus said, "Big Toby, are you absolutely, positively certain the man you saw at the hotel tonight is the same man who knocked down the fellow from the saloon?"

Toby placed his hand over his heart. "As God is my witness, Mr. McAdams, he was the same man."

Lavinia exchanged glances with her father and Huck, then asked Big Toby, "Do you remember anything else about this man besides the fact that he was big? Did you notice the color of his hair, or eyes?"

Big Toby nodded. "His hair was blond, like mine. But he didn't have too much of it. He was nearly bald. And I remember his eyes. They were light blue. I could never forget that. When he grabbed me by the shirt, he gave me the meanest stare I've ever seen. His blue eyes seemed to be on fire!"

Angus thought a moment. "He sure sounds like the fellow I hired today, but he claimed he was from Pittsburgh." To Big Toby, he said, "Have you had any supper yet?"

The boy shook his head. "I'm not hungry."

Lavinia said, "Not even for a piece of Grandma's wild blueberry cake?"

"Cake?" Big Toby's eyebrows rose. "I just might be able to put away a piece of cake."

Angus smiled. "Good. We'll set a place for you at the table, and when Grandma cuts the cake, she'll serve you some." Angus rose, starting toward the dining room.

Lavinia, Huck, and Big Toby followed him out of the parlor, but Big Toby stopped abruptly in the hallway.

"Mr. McAdams, what about that big man?"

Angus put a reassuring hand on his shoulder. "After supper, I'll go down and have a talk with him. It will all work out."

Lines of skepticism marred the boy's forehead, but he argued no further. A place was quickly set at the table for him, and the ham and potatoes passed. Refusing them at first, he managed to consume a small portion of each after Little Toby informed him of the dinnertime rule—he would be served no dessert unless he had first eaten some meat and potatoes.

Conversation soon turned to the new room and when the main course had ended, Lavinia helped her grandmother cut the unfrosted cake with the wild blueberry filling. They topped each piece with a dollop of freshly whipped cream and a few berries. The sweet filling intermingled with the richness of the cream made a delectable summer treat.

When all had enjoyed their portion, Angus said, "Now, Grandma, are you ready to see your room?"

A wide smile lit her face. "Ready as I'll ever be!"

Chapter

10

Lavinia and the rest of the family followed Angus as he led Grandma through the kitchen to the closed door of her new room. On it hung a sign draped with a cloth. Angus pointed to it, saying, "The first order of business is to unveil your sign."

Grandma whisked the cloth away, revealing a large plaque cut into the shape of a maple leaf. Across the center, fancily etched letters spelled the word "Welcome". Grandma turned to Huck with a smile. "I know your work when I see it. Thank you for the beautiful sign, Huck!"

"My pleasure!" he replied with a smile.

Angus pulled a skeleton key from his pocket and handed it to Grandma. "Go ahead! Unlock your door!"

Her hand trembled when she turned the key. Grasping the knob, she unlatched the door and opened it wide. Her hands flew to her cheeks.

"Oh, my! Oh, my!" She started to sway.

Angus put his arms around her. "Huck, fetch a chair, will you?"

He swiftly brought a black straight chair that had been painted with golden maple leaves on its back and placed it behind her.

Angus eased Grandma onto the chair, and Lavinia could see the tears welling in her eyes as she took in the sight before her.

Flora asked eagerly, "Do you like it, Grandma?"

She dabbed the moisture from her eyes with the corner of her apron and turned to the girl. "I more than like it, child. I'm *wild* about it!" Gaining her composure, and her feet, she began to tour the room of wainscoting and plaster, stopping first at the new wardrobe that stood against the wall to her right. She paused to run her finger over the maple leaves etched into the door. "This is more of Huck's fine work, isn't it?"

He smiled. "Yes, ma'am. I hope it meets your approval."

Toby said, "Papa and I built this wardrobe, Grandma."

Angus said, "Now you know why we didn't catch many fish. If they didn't start biting right away, we went over to the carpenters' shed and worked on this instead."

"It's the finest wardrobe I ever did see," she assured them. Moving toward one of the maple leaves that had been set into each corner of the hardwood floor, she said, "I've never seen a floor as fancy as this one. Did you build this in the carpenters' shed, too?"

Angus chuckled. "I had to do a lot of talking with the carpenters before I convinced one of them to put in the maple leaves."

"God bless him!" Grandma exclaimed. Pointing to the hooked rug alongside the bed against the back wall, she asked, "Whose effort went into the maple leaf on my new rug?"

Flora said, "Alice and Grace's mama made it."

Grandma moved closer, running her toe over the closely spaced green loops of the background, and the higher golden loops that comprised the leaf. "Alice and Grace's mama did a fine job," she concluded, her gaze rising to the quilt that covered her bed. It was hand sewn with a maple leaf in every square, in calicoes ranging from green to amber to red. She ran her hand over it affectionately. "My quilt never looked finer than it does right here in this room." She reached for one of the three pillows leaning against the back wall. "And these pillows go perfectly, with a big maple leaf at the center of each."

Mary said, "Lavinia and I sewed them for you. I remember the five years you took to make this quilt, and how you've cherished it. I thought it only right to plan the pillows and all the rest to complement it."

Grandma smiled and moved on to the curtains. They hung straight to the sill, completely concealing the back window for now, but were designed with tiebacks. She ran her hand over the cotton fabric. "Even these new curtains are bordered with maple leaves, and would you look at this!" She pointed to one of the pair of tieback fixtures that sported a maple leaf on its face.

Lavinia said, "That was my idea. Papa made those from a pattern I drew."

Little Toby said, "And I sanded them and varnished them."

Grandma grinned. "This is one clever, maple-minded family." Her focus rose to the simple maple leaf border stenciled just below the ceiling. "Who painted that?"

Big Toby said, "I did! My Aunt Edna taught me how to stencil last fall. Now, she has ivy all around her kitchen."

"She taught you well," Grandma concluded, heading for a rocker that had a maple leaf design on its chair pad. "I think I might just sit down here a while and gaze upon this wonderful new room."

Mary stepped toward the back window. "I have one more surprise for you, Mother."

"What's that, dear?" Grandma asked, turning her chair

to face her daughter before sitting down.

Mary drew the curtains aside to reveal a nine pane window. In the very center was a pane of stained glass designed with an amber maple leaf in the center and pale green glass for the background.

Grandma gasped. "It's the window from my breakfast nook! My favorite in the whole, wide world! How did you ever convince that irascible brother of yours to send it up here?"

"I didn't," Mary replied. "I wrote to the man who made it and asked him to make another exactly like it and ship it up here. It will catch the morning sun, just like the one at home."

"Bless your heart, dear!" Grandma replied. "Bless *all* your hearts for making this the best room I have ever seen in my entire life. Thank you!"

Angus said, "You're welcome. Now, if you'll excuse me, I'd better get over to the hotel and see that new man like I promised Big Toby. I'll be back soon."

When he had gone, the others settled on chairs in Grandma's new room except for Mary, who began to clean up the dinner dishes. Big Toby began telling Grandma, Little Toby, and Flora his story about the big man, and had just concluded when a loud knock sounded at the door. He jumped up with fright. "That's him! I know it! I've got to get out of here!"

Flora ran to the parlor window, calling to the others, "It's only Mr. O'Connell, and Alice and Grace! And they've brought Cubby!" She hurried to the door.

Lavinia joined Flora to welcome the O'Connells, as did everyone but Big Toby and Huck, who stayed back to calm the anxious boy.

Mary greeted the O'Connells cordially. "How nice of

you to stop by! Do come in!"

Mr. O'Connell shook his head. "I thank you for your hospitality, Mrs. McAdams, but I dare not pass over your doorstep with this mischievous fellow." He patted the cub who had grown sufficiently in the past three months to wear a rope leash about his neck.

Flora reached for her pet. "I'll take him, Mr. O'Connell."

"Hold tight, darlin', he's a terror when he's loose," he warned, placing the cub in her arms.

In a flash the wily fellow had wiggled free, taking off down the road, rope dragging behind.

"Cubby! Come back!" Flora cried, running after him. Little Toby, Alice, and Grace followed.

Mr. O'Connell told Mary and Grandma, "I canna' keep the cub any longer. He's taken to stealing the eggs from under my hens!"

Mary nodded in understanding.

Mr. O'Connell continued. "If he were mine, I'd take him out to Big Summer Island, I would. It'd stop him from raiding the coops hereabouts. But for now, build him a pen that'll hold him tight or you'll be missing your morning eggs!"

By the time he had given his advice, Little Toby, Flora, Alice, and Grace had returned with Cubby, who showed far more aptitude for playing with his leash and chewing on it, than being led by it.

Mary told Flora, "Take Cubby around back. Tie him to a tree, and stay by him until Papa comes home."

"Yes, Mama." She hurried off to do as asked, Alice and Grace with her.

To Little Toby, Grandma said, "You'd better go and help the girls. And whatever you do, make sure that cub doesn't get loose!"

"Yes, ma'am."

When he had gone, Mary told Mr. O'Connell, "I'm sorry for the loss of your eggs. I'd like to make it up to you." To Lavinia, she said, "Fetch the jar where we keep our spare coins, please."

Mr. O'Connell shook his head. "No need! But there *is* something you can do for me."

"What might that be?" Mary asked.

"Shamrock's pups need homes. Your youngsters 'd make right good companions to one of 'em."

"I'll give it some thought," Mary replied.

Grandma told Mr. O'Connell, "That's no small payment you ask in return for the eggs Flora's cub stole. Raising a pup is a big chore." To Mary, she said, "You'd be far better off paying him for his loss."

Lavinia said, "I think Flora and Little Toby would welcome the chore of raising a pup. And the dog would be a good companion to you, too, Grandma!"

She scowled. "A puppy will ruin your nicest things!"

Mary returned her attention to Mr. O'Connell. "Like I said, I'll give your suggestion some thought. First, we have to get Cubby off on his own."

Mr. O'Connell said, "I'll check with you later about the pup, then. Good evening, ladies!" He called Alice and Grace, then headed down the road, hand in hand with his daughters.

While Mary and Grandma headed for the kitchen to wash up the dinner dishes, Lavinia went to the parlor where Huck and Big Toby were now seated. Huck was still trying to convince Big Toby that he was in no imminent danger from the new, big man in town. "He worked at the casting house all afternoon, and showed nary a hint of ill temper, even when his barrow tipped and lost its load. He just laughed and loaded it up again—all twenty-two pigs."

Lavinia said, "Besides, he told Papa he's from Pittsburgh, not Marquette."

Big Toby argued. "If I'd killed a man in Marquette, I'd say I was from somewhere else, too. He's from Marquette, all right. I know it for a certainty!"

The discussion continued for several more minutes with Big Toby still unconvinced when Angus arrived home from the hotel. He joined them in the parlor, a confident smile in place. "Big Toby, you can go back to the hotel without a single doubt in your mind that the big man there is *not* the one you saw in Marquette."

"How can you be so sure, Mr. McAdams?"

"I had quite a talk with him. He told me about his relatives in Pittsburgh and gave me further information about his former employer. He can't write more than his own name, so he couldn't put down their addresses for me to check, but from the details he shared, I'm certain his words are true. Meanwhile, Mr. Rose is looking for you. There's a load of dinner dishes just waiting to be washed and put away!"

Big Toby wrung his hands. "I don't know if I can go back, Mr. McAdams. I just don't know."

"I'll go with you, if you want." Angus started to rise.

The boy jumped to his feet and put out a staying hand. "No need. Good night, and thanks for supper!" He took off like a flash, the front door closing with a thud behind him.

Angus shook his head in puzzlement. "You just never can tell about that boy."

Mary came into the parlor, her gaze on Angus. "I'm glad you're back. I have an important job for you." She explained about Cubby, asking, "Can you build him a cage to sleep in tonight?"

Angus rose. "There should be enough scrap lumber left over from Grandma's room to do the job."

Huck said, "I'll help."

Lavinia followed them to the back yard where her brother and sister were nearly at wit's end to keep Cubby from chewing through his rope leash. While Toby helped his father and Huck with construction of a cage, Lavinia helped Flora watch over her pet. The playful little fellow, though cute in appearance with his keen brown eyes, little stand-up ears, and small black nose, was constantly testing his needle-like teeth. He nipped incessantly at fingers, clothing, sticks—anything within reach of his pointed little mouth, and no amount of scolding could deter him. After more than an hour of tussling with the little creature, and with dusk settling in, the cage was finally ready. It had slits between the boards wide enough for air circulation but too narrow for escape. A rope fastened to two exterior cleats served as a lock.

Flora set Cubby inside the box and tied the door shut, telling him, "This is your new home! I hope you like it!"

He scratched at the sides and yapped with disapproval.

She spoke to him through a slit in the top. "I'm sorry you have to stay in a cage, but it's only for the night. I'll come and let you out in the morning. I promise!"

Angus lay a hand on her shoulder. "It's getting late, little one. Say good night and go up to bed."

"Good night, Cubby!" She started for the back door.

He whined, and she paused, then headed inside.

Huck took Lavinia's hands in his. "I'd better be on my way. I'll see you tomorrow after supper, if I may?"

Angus said, "Won't you come inside for a cup of tea? It's the least I can offer in return for your help."

Lavinia said, "I'm sure Grandma must have a couple of sugar cookies hidden away to go with it."

Huck smiled. "I could never refuse Grandma's cookies!"

In the parlor, while waiting for the tea to steep, conversation grew difficult, distracted as Huck and Lavinia were by the protestations of Cubby whose whines and howls penetrated the night air, drifting in through wide open windows. Lavinia lowered them, leaving about six inches to allow a refreshing breeze to circulate, but Cubby's unhappy sounds continued to haunt them. He hadn't quieted any a half-hour later when Huck rose to take his leave. Lavinia saw him to the front door where he turned to her again, his gaze settling affectionately on her as he took her hand in his.

"I hope you'll be able to sleep. I don't mind saying I'm glad that little fellow isn't caged outside my window for the night."

Lavinia smiled. "If he keeps me awake, I'll simply set my thoughts on the most pleasant subject I know. You!"

Huck squeezed her hand, wanting to taste the sweet smile on her lips. But he knew such affection must wait until betrothal, and betrothal must wait until he was certain that she would accept him. These last two months of calling on Lavinia had passed with hardly a ruffle between them, and she hadn't once mentioned the prospect of returning to Canada upon her seventeenth birthday, but he mustn't press her just yet.

Lavinia studied the tenderness in Huck's blue-eyed gaze and felt herself melting in its warmth. With the passing of each evening together, he had managed to dissolve a portion of her icy resolve never to marry a furnace man. Now, not even an ice chip remained. Little by little he had conquered her heart, but she wouldn't admit it to him yet. Soon, but not yet.

Huck enfolded her hand in both of his. "I'll call on you tomorrow, if I may?"

Lavinia smiled brightly, her eyes sparkling. "You not only may, you had better, or I will be bitterly disappointed!"

"Until tomorrow, then," he promised, heading out the door.

In a state of pure elation, Lavinia returned to the parlor to collect their teacups. She remembered when the only thing she could think of was the day when she would leave Fayette. But those thoughts were nearly gone, chased off by Huck's winning ways. Now, she couldn't help dreaming of a time to come when she would be so certain of her love for Huck and his love for her that she would be promised to him. Then, she would be dancing on air! But for now, she needed to keep her feet on the floor and head them in the direction of the kitchen. While washing teacups and saucers, she heard her folks in conversation with Grandma in her new room. Grandma was talking.

"No one's going to get a wink of sleep tonight, the way that fox cub is carrying on."

Angus said, "He'll go to sleep, eventually."

Mary said, "I wouldn't count on it. Do you remember that spaniel puppy Papa brought home when I was a girl, Mama?"

Grandma grumbled. "How could I forget? He tore up three of my finest quilts before he got his second teeth."

Mary said, "But he turned into a fine companion, and when he died twelve years later, you sorely missed him."

"I did," Grandma admitted, "but I won't miss the noise that cub is making when he finally quits, *if* he quits."

Angus said, "Maybe Cubby will quiet down if I move his cage into the girls' room."

Mary said, "It's certainly worth a try. I'll help you."

Grandma said, "Put an old towel in his cage. He misses his littermates. It will give him something to cuddle up to."

Lavinia was putting away the last of the clean dishes when her folks came through the kitchen carrying Cubby's cage. She fetched an old towel and followed them upstairs. The move to a spot at the foot of Flora's bed, and the addition of the towel for comfort seemed to quiet the cub. Lavinia washed up, changed to her nightgown, dowsed the lamp, and crawled into bed. Then Cubby's whimpering started up again.

Toby scolded him loudly from the next room.

Flora got up out of bed and sat beside the crate to talk to the little fox, but he would not be consoled by human words. To Lavinia, she said, "I'm going to bring him up on my bed. Maybe then, he'll sleep."

"You'd better ask Mama first," she warned, but when Flora put Cubby and his towel on her bed and he instantly quieted down, Lavinia said nothing further, drifting quickly into a deep and satisfying sleep.

She was still in dreamland when the furnace whistle roused her in the dusk of early morning. She could hear the rustling of Flora's sheet on the bed next to hers, then the panic in her little sister's voice.

"Livvy! Cubby's gone!"

Chapter

11

Suddenly wide-awake, Lavinia pressed her feet to the cool wooden floor, telling Flora, "I'll light the lantern and help you look for Cubby."

Lavinia prayed for guidance. Finding no sign of him in their bedroom or Toby's, they headed downstairs where their mother and grandmother remained at the dining table after their father had gone to work. Flora burst into the room.

"Mama! Grandma! Have you seen Cubby?"

Mary offered a puzzled look. "Isn't he in his cage?"

Flora shook her head.

Grandma said, "Don't tell me you let him out!"

Flora burst into tears. "I didn't mean to lose him . . . I just wanted him to be quiet . . . so I let him sleep on my bed. Now he's gone!"

Mary went to Flora and put her arms about her. "There, there, child. Calm yourself. We'll find him. Are you sure he isn't upstairs?"

Lavinia said, "We looked everywhere up there. We hoped he was down here with you."

Grandma said, "We haven't seen hide nor hair of him, but that doesn't mean he's left the house."

Mary wiped the tears from Flora's cheeks and took her by the hand. "Come, dear. We'll look under every piece of furniture and in every corner of every room. Maybe he's found himself a den and curled up somewhere."

The hunt resumed until every square inch of the first floor had been thoroughly searched, ending in the parlor.

Mary pointed to the parlor window, still open several inches as Lavinia had left it the night before. "I suspect he jumped up on that sill and escaped out the window."

Flora headed for the stairs. "I'm going to get dressed and go look for him!"

"Not so fast!" Mary warned. "After you get dressed, you will sit down for breakfast. When you have eaten, you may have ten minutes to search this neighborhood for Cubby. Then, whether you've found him or not, you and Lavinia and Toby will help with chores. While we were looking for Cubby, I noticed that the dust from construction is worse than I thought. Now that Grandma's room is complete, we're going to give the rest of this house a thorough cleaning."

"But, Mama—"

"But, nothing! Now go and do as I say. And stop worrying about Cubby. If you don't find him, I expect he'll turn up later at the O'Connells' and Alice and Grace will bring him here. After all, he's been getting some pretty good breakfasts there according to Mr. O'Connell!"

Near tears again, Flora started up the stairs. Lavinia followed. She tried to comfort her little sister, speaking words of assurance that Cubby would be found before the day was spent, but Flora remained troubled, hugging the precious dolly that Grandma had given her on her birthday. When Lavinia had helped Flora with the buttons on the back of her dress and braided her hair, she sent Flora downstairs and started on her own morning routine. While washing up, combing her hair, and putting on her gray flannel dress for the housework that was ahead, she prayed that Flora would find Cubby after breakfast. As she was buttoning her dress, a light breeze blew in the open window, ruffling the curtain. It carried with it the scent of furnace smoke and the song of the robins, sparrows, and wrens. Then the crack of shotgun fire rent the air, giving her a start. Silence followed and Lavinia wondered who could be shooting off a gun in town at this hour of the morning? When no answer came to mind, she dismissed the idle question, headed downstairs, and tucked into the delicious flapjack her grandmother set before her. The fish-shaped pancake swam in a pool of golden maple syrup that would satisfy even the most voracious appetite for sweets, and reminded her of the animal pancakes and syrup her grandmother had served her when she was a child in Canada. But this morning, with concern high over Cubby, and Flora barely eating, Lavinia's favorite breakfast turned bittersweet.

The meal over and the ten-minute search for Cubby unfruitful, housework began. While Mary enlisted Toby's help to clean the master bedroom, Lavinia and Flora started in the dining room. The work consumed Lavinia's attention, and helped distract Flora from her worries. Rags in hand, they thoroughly wiped every speck of dust from the walls, floor, and furniture, and then headed to the parlor. They were hard at work there when a knock came at the door. Flora hurried to answer, admitting Alice and Grace who asked if she could come out to play, but they carried no fox cub with them.

Ignoring their question, Flora immediately blurted out the foremost thought on her mind. "Have you seen Cubby? He ran away!"

The girls shook their heads in unison, then Alice said, "We haven't seen him since we left here last night."

Mary and Toby joined the girls, and Flora turned to her

mother in earnest. "Mama, Cubby didn't go back to O'Connells'. I've *got* to go look for him again!"

"Not now, Flora."

"Mama, *please!*" Flora begged.

Mary placed her hands on her daughter's shoulders and looked her straight on. "You must tend to your chores this morning, helping your sister with the cleaning. Then, if all is spotless by the time we eat our midday meal, we'll look for Cubby this afternoon. Perhaps Alice and Grace will come back then to help us."

The O'Connell girls quickly agreed and took their leave, then Flora headed back to the parlor, chin low.

Lavinia put her arm about her sister's shoulders. "We're sure to find him later on, Flora. He can't have roamed far. After all, he's only three months old."

Flora gazed up with liquid eyes. "I sure hope you're right, Livvy."

Their work continued, clearing dust from the parlor walls, furniture, and floor, the entryway, and the upstairs bedrooms. Lavinia told stories to Flora as they worked, trying to distract her from troubling thoughts about Cubby, and attempting to forget how hot the day was becoming, but with little success. Flora was still glum and dispirited when the midday dinner whistle blew, and Lavinia was looking forward to splashing her moist face with cool water from the well. Mary came upstairs to inspect the cleaning effort, a smile of approval evident.

"The parlor looks wonderful, and the upstairs is in fine shape, too, thanks to you girls!" Her arm about Flora's shoulders, she said, "You know what that means—after dinner we'll *all* go and look for Cubby. Now, will you and Lavinia please wash up and set the table? Your father will be home any minute."

Flora gave a nod, picked up her new dolly and clutched her tight, then set her back in her rocker and headed downstairs, minus her usual enthusiasm. Lavinia and her mother followed, exchanging glances that made words unnecessary. They were in for a difficult time with the sullen Flora unless Cubby could be found.

A few minutes later, Angus walked in the front door. Flora abandoned her table-setting chore to greet him, as did Lavinia. Flora immediately explained about the missing Cubby.

Angus told Flora, "I'm sure you'll find him, honey, with all the help you'll have."

Mary came to greet her husband with a kiss on the cheek. "You and Toby had better wash for dinner." To Lavinia and Flora, she said, "And if you girls don't finish setting the table in the next two minutes, your grandmother will be mighty displeased. Her roasted chicken is ready to come out of the oven."

In a flurry of activity, the flatware, dinnerware, and napkins appeared in proper arrangement. Everyone took a seat at the table, and Angus carved the chicken and passed the potatoes and peas.

The chicken was so tender it fell off the bones and melted in Lavinia's mouth, imparting its delicious, roasted flavor—slightly salty, slightly sweet. She hoped she would be able to serve as pleasing a bird someday when she was married and on her own. She longed to be the recipient of Huck's enthusiastic compliments, like the ones her grandmother was now receiving from her father. So tasty was the dinner that few words were spoken until her father had finished his chicken and reached for a slice of bread.

While spreading it with butter, he said, "I'm afraid Cubby isn't the only one who came up missing today.

When I got to the furnace this morning, Huck told me that Big Toby has disappeared. Not a soul has seen him since he left our place last night."

Mary said, "He must have been too scared of that new man to return to the hotel."

Angus said, "I just don't understand it. The new fellow is good-humored—almost jolly. He certainly doesn't seem the type to cause trouble the way Big Toby said."

Lavinia asked, "Where do you suppose Big Toby's gone?"

Angus shrugged. "It's anyone's guess."

Mary said, "I hope he'll be all right. He wasn't doing well at all when he showed up here a couple of months ago on the shoulders of Big Billy Bassett."

Grandma said, "I think Big Toby's gone back to his Aunt Edna."

Flora said, "He won't go back there! He ran away from her!"

Toby said, "Like Cubby ran away from you?"

Mary shot warning glances at Flora and Toby. "Careful, you two, or you'll spend the rest of the day in your rooms!"

After a moment's silence, Angus said, "Mr. Rose is lost without Big Toby to wash dishes and tend to the other chores at the hotel."

Toby said meekly, "Papa, I could help Mr. Rose, if you'd let me. After all, I'm twelve years old now and a lot smarter than Big Toby. I'm sure I could do just as good a job as he did."

Mary said, "You're forgetting that come September, you'll have your studies to tend to and you won't be able to work there during the day."

Toby said, "I know, but I could work all summer." His gaze on his father, he said, "Please, Papa, may I at least try?"

Angus said, "Come with me after dinner, son. We'll stop by the hotel and you may make your suggestion to Mr. Rose yourself."

"Thanks, Papa!"

Mary said, "Not so fast, you two!" She focused on Toby. "If Mr. Rose hires you, you'll be home by sunset each night. Understand?"

"Yes, ma'am!"

Flora asked Toby, "Does that mean you're not going to help us look for Cubby?"

He shrugged. "If Mr. Rose has a job for me this afternoon, then you'll have to find Cubby without me."

Flora looked crestfallen. "But I need you! I need all the help I can get!"

Lavinia said, "Flora, don't fret. You'll have plenty of help whether Toby comes with us, or not."

Flora sighed, stabbing half-heartedly at a morsel of chicken on her plate.

When the meal had come to an end and Angus and Toby had left, the O'Connell girls returned, reporting that they had searched the shanty village and found no sign of Cubby there. Mary suggested that the four girls start by going to each of the houses up the road in the direction of the Harris's, promising that she would help them search the woods if they hadn't found Cubby by the time they'd gone door to door.

Lavinia set out with the younger girls, feeling the heat of the afternoon sun that glared down from a brilliant blue sky. At the first few homes, Flora's inquiry met with the same response. No one had seen a fox cub. Next, they arrived at Dr. Sloane's. He answered their knock with a smile.

"Good afternoon, children! What brings you to my door? You look too healthy to need doctoring!"

Flora almost smiled. "We're not sick. We're looking for something. Have you seen a fox cub about this long and this tall?" She demonstrated Cubby's size. "He's my pet, and he ran away last night."

Dr. Sloane thought a moment, his smile gone. Then a less convincing form of it reappeared when he told Flora, "Maybe he's gone back to his mama in the woods."

She shook her head vigorously. "His mama's dead. Somebody shot her right after Cubby was born. Alice and Grace and Moira raised him until he came to live with me last night, but he ran away. I've got to find him!"

"I see," Dr. Sloane said, scratching his chin. "Sorry I can't help you."

Lavinia said, "Thanks, anyway, Dr. Sloane. I guess we'll go on to the Harris's and ask there."

They had turned to go when Dr. Sloane said, "Wait!" His focus clearly on Lavinia, he asked, "May I see you a moment?" Drawing her into the entryway, he closed the door and spoke in hushed tones. "I think I know what happened to your little sister's fox cub." With sadness in his eyes and regret in his voice, he explained. "I heard a ruckus in my chicken coop early this morning, so I grabbed my shotgun and went to see what was wrong. A fox cub about the size of your sister's was stirring up my hens, so I killed him and buried him. I didn't know he was someone's pet. I'm sorry."

Lavinia knew now that the crack of shotgun fire she had heard when she was getting dressed had signaled the death of Cubby. The realization sent a rock to the pit of her stomach. She wanted to lash out at Dr. Sloane, but she knew full well that she couldn't blame him for bringing Cubby to such an abrupt end. She drew a deep breath and prayed for the right words.

"Thank you for telling me, Dr. Sloane. Good day." She stepped outside the door to join the others.

Flora said anxiously, "Come on, Livvy. Let's go to the Harris's. Maybe they've seen Cubby. It's the only house in the neighborhood that we haven't been to yet."

With a nod, Lavinia agreed to the suggestion, deciding to wait until she could enlist the help of her mother to explain the bad news to Flora. When both Mrs. Harris and her hired woman, Marian, said they had not seen Cubby, the girls headed home. Feeling the heat of the day pressing upon them, they headed straight to the well pump, and Lavinia worked the handle hard and fast, splashing water into the tin cup kept there for times such as this. She took a few sips then passed the cup to the others, saying, "I'll go get Mama." A couple of minutes later, they came out the back door together.

Flora tossed off the water left in the cup, hung it on the spout, and said, "Come on, Mama! Let's go look in the woods for Cubby!"

Taking a seat on the upper back step, Mary said, "Flora, come and sit here, beside me, please. I want to talk to you first."

"But—"

"Come!" Mary insisted.

Reluctantly, Flora sat beside her mother. Lavinia and the O'Connell twins sat on the step below.

Mary took Flora's hand in hers. "Darling, there's no need to search the woods. Cubby's not there."

"How do you know?" Flora challenged.

"I'm sorry to have to tell you this, dear, but Dr. Sloane told Lavinia that he buried Cubby this morning."

"No! It isn't true!" Flora turned to her sister. "Livvy, tell Mama it isn't so!"

Lavinia shook her head. "I'm sorry, Flora. Cubby got into Dr. Sloane's hen house this morning, so he took his shotgun and—"

"No!" Flora cried. "He's in the woods! I just know it!" Tears streaming down her face, she leaped from the step and ran off into the woods as fast as her legs could carry her.

Chapter

12

"Flora! Come back!" Lavinia shouted, lifting her skirt to run after her sister.

With the help of the O'Connell twins, she and her mother soon located the heartsick little girl curled up in a ball and sobbing hysterically at the foot of a maple.

Lavinia sat down, placing a soothing arm about her sister's trembling shoulders. "Flora, I'm sorry you're so upset. Let's go home and get one of Grandma's sugar cookies."

With great gulps, she cried, "No! I don't want a cookie . . . I want *Cubby!*"

Mary knelt down, her words silken with sympathy. "I'm sorry Cubby's gone, dear, but crying won't bring him back. Please come home. You can't stay here all day."

"Yes . . . I can!" Flora challenged between sobs.

Alice sat down beside her friend. "Flora, now that Cubby's gone, maybe your mother will let you have one of Shamrock's pups."

Mary nodded. "That's a fine idea, don't you think, Flora?"

"No!" Flora instantly replied.

Grace asked, "Are you sure you don't want a puppy? If Cubby were still alive, you would have had to take him to an island soon, but a puppy will be your friend for his whole life."

Flora looked up, pondering Grace's words, then sobbed some more.

Mary told Lavinia, "Stay with Flora for a spell, will you?" To Alice and Grace, she said, "Come with me, please."

Lavinia remained beside Flora, who sobbed herself into weariness, then lay her head on Lavinia's lap and closed her eyes. Lavinia stroked Flora's hair, silently seeking God's comforting hand in the matter, then she leaned back against the tree trunk and allowed the heat of the day to lull her into semi-sleep. She was unsure how long she had been dozing when she heard a rustling in the woods nearby, then looked up to find Alice, Grace, and her mother who was holding a rope leash attached to one of Shamrock's offspring.

The copper-colored puppy immediately started licking Flora's face. She tried to push him away, but the puppy persisted, then started nipping Flora's hand with his sharp teeth.

"Ouch! Stop that!" Flora ordered, wrapping her hand about the puppy's short snout.

Mary asked, "What will you call him, Flora?"

Alice said, "Think of a name!"

Grace said, "How about Stubby? He hasn't much for a nose or tail, and he's rather short and plump."

Flora almost smiled. "Stubby. That's his name."

Mary said, "Stubby it is, then. Now, Stubby is hungry and thirsty. Let's take him home and give him something to eat and drink." She handed the leash to Flora.

Without a single word of protest, the little girl rose to her feet and led the dog home. By the time she arrived, she had grown thoroughly enthusiastic for her new pet, and rushed inside to introduce him to Grandma.

"This is my new puppy, Stubby!" she announced with pride.

The elderly woman paused in her sewing to gaze skeptically at the new family member who was sniffing at the hem of her skirt. "Stubby, eh? Are you sure that's the right name for him? Perhaps you should call him 'Trouble', for that's sure to come with a pup his age."

At that very instant, Stubby took the hem of her skirt in his teeth and began tugging this way and that.

"Leave it!" Grandma sharply commanded, placing one hand over Stubby's snout and pulling his lower jaw down with the other to release the fabric of her skirt. Then she lifted Stubby into the air, gazed into his brown eyes, and said, "If you and I are going to get along, you're going to have to learn to chew only on your own toy. I'll make you one right now." She set Stubby down and focused on Flora. "Have you any worn out clothes with your scent on them that I can fashion a toy from?"

Flora shook her head. "My old clothes are all washed and clean."

Lavinia asked, "What about the towel from Cubby's cage? It smells like Cubby, but it smells like Flora, too."

Grandma said, "That might be just the thing. It will remind Stubby of his old friend. Flora, go and fetch it for me, will you please?"

While Flora was gone, Mary brought a bowl of water for Stubby. He lapped eagerly.

When Flora returned with the towel, Grandma told her, "Now, take Stubby and his bowl of water out back. I'll make his chew toy."

Mary said, "And I'll fix a dish of food for him."

"Thank you, Mama, Grandma!" Flora said gaily, leading her puppy toward the back door. The O'Connell twins followed, Alice carrying the water bowl.

When the youngsters had gone, Grandma told Mary, "You shouldn't have given the girl the puppy. She'll think she can have anything her heart desires if she cries long enough. You're spoiling her."

"And I suppose you're *not*, baking sugar cookies each and every time she asks," Mary replied. When a tense moment had lapsed, she continued. "Flora wasn't crying because she wanted a puppy. She was crying because her heart was broken over Cubby."

Lavinia said, "That's right, Grandma. Flora had no idea Mama was going to give her the puppy today."

"It is a decision we will all surely come to regret in short order," Grandma said tersely. "See to it that the pup stays out of my room. I want nothing more to do with it once I've finished making this chew toy." She commenced ripping the towel into strips.

Mary turned on her heel and headed for the kitchen.

Lavinia followed. As she helped to fill a dish with scraps of bread and fat for Stubby, she could see the strain on her mother's face. Eager to exit the kitchen, she said, "I'll take the dish out to Stubby."

Her mother nodded and reached for a mixing bowl. "I think I'll bake some taffy tarts. I haven't made them once since Mother arrived and commenced to filling our cookie jar with an endless supply of sugar cookies. Besides, we could do with a little celebration at supper tonight. Flora has a puppy and Toby evidently has a new job. Would you please bring some wood and light the stove?"

"Sure, Mama."

Lavinia delivered the dish to Stubby, then gathered the wood. But when she was passing through her grandmother's room on the way to the kitchen, the elderly woman's sharp inquiry brought her up short.

"Lavinia, what are you doing with that wood?"

After a moment's hesitation, she calmly explained, "I'm

147

going to light the stove so Mama can bake taffy tarts."

Grandma dropped the half-finished chew toy she was making into her sewing basket and nearly sprang from her rocker, spry steps carrying her to the kitchen just ahead of Lavinia.

Mary was measuring flour by the cupful into the bowl when her mother confronted her. "You can't bake tarts now! I'm going to need the oven soon for my casserole." To Lavinia, she said, "Put that wood by the stove. I'll be in soon to light it."

Lavinia could hear the tension in her mother's voice when she said sternly, "Lavinia, light the stove *now*, please."

Grandma told her, "You'll do no such thing!"

Mary's cheeks flushed. "Mother, this is *my* kitchen, and Lavinia is *my* daughter. Stop interfering!"

"*You're* the one who's interfering!" Grandma claimed. "We made an agreement that I'm in charge of cooking the meals. Now, you're—"

Lavinia cut in. "Grandma! Mama! You sound worse than a couple of bickering children!" Dropping the wood into the wood box with a clatter, she headed for her room to wash up and put on her blue dress, saying, "I surely hope you'll work out your differences before Huck comes to call, or you'll embarrass me half to death!"

But when supper was served an hour later than usual, tension still ran high and a frigid silence had settled in between her mother and grandmother. Lavinia was at the dining table finishing the last of the casserole along with the rest of her family—except Toby who was washing dishes at the hotel—when Huck's knock sounded at the front door.

Lavinia rose to answer the door, her father saying, "Invite Huck to join us at the table for dessert. He may sit at Toby's place."

She would have preferred to skip the tarts and invite Huck into the parlor, free of the frosty atmosphere at the table, but she dared not counter her father's request. Reluctantly, she rose from the table, issuing a silent prayer on her way to the door. *Lord, let Thy warmth thaw the ice, and do it now!*

When she and Huck had been seated, Grandma wasted no time informing him, "We'd have finished dinner an hour ago, except Mary decided late this afternoon to bake a batch of taffy tarts." She gave her daughter a sideways glance. "In so doing, she delayed the preparation of my casserole." The corner of her mouth tilting upward, she added warmly, "Of course, the delay is all to your advantage. My daughter bakes the best taffy tarts either side of the border, as you're about to discover."

"I've already made that discovery," Huck swiftly replied. While he recounted the occasion on the rainy night back in April when he had come to deliver the slates for the scholars, Mary went to fetch the dessert plates and a platter of her freshly baked tarts.

When everyone had been served, Flora began telling him about her day—the search for Cubby, the bad news from Dr. Sloane, and the acquisition of Stubby, now crated in the back yard under a shade tree.

After several minutes of meticulous detail about her marvelous new pet, Huck asked, "Are you planning to take Stubby for a walk after supper?"

Flora shrugged. "I hadn't thought about it."

Angus said, "I think it's a grand idea." To Lavinia, he said, "I'd like you and Huck to go along and make sure Flora's new pet doesn't get into any mischief."

"Yes, Papa," Lavinia replied, looking forward to a stroll

in the cooler outdoor air before darkness would send them indoors. A few minutes later they were headed up the road in the direction of the Sloane and Harris homes, then around the curve and along the road that overlooked the lake. It was particularly calm tonight, an intense shade of aqua blue that gave it a warm, inviting feeling. But no breeze stirred the warm, muggy atmosphere.

Huck said, "Let's go up to the bluff. Maybe the air is moving up there."

Flora said, "We could stop by the O'Connells' on the way and Stubby can say hello to his mama."

Lavinia shook her head. "Stubby needs to get used to his new family. He'll get confused if you keep taking him back to his old home."

"All right," Flora reluctantly agreed, but she understood better when Stubby instinctively pulled in the direction of his old home when they passed through the heart of town.

On the trail to the bluff, Lavinia couldn't help remembering the first time she'd been there and the view of the harbor and village that had enthralled her. When they arrived at the opening with the stump seats where she and Huck had sat and talked, she paused again to rest and take in the panorama. Huck sat beside her, and Flora and Stubby settled on the grass at their feet. A cooling breeze stirred, and within moments, Stubby lay asleep on Flora's lap while she leaned back against her sister's skirt and dozed off.

Lavinia gazed out across the harbor and beyond to the bay and shoreline farther west. She delighted in the red ball that had been hung in the sky by the hand of the Almighty. The fiery orb descended toward a horizon of orange and pink. Closer in, the village itself appeared as enchanting as it had before, only more so at this time of the evening. In a voice barely above a whisper, she told Huck, "When I look down at the village and harbor, I can't help thinking about Palemon and Lavinia—the one from the poem that I'm named for. I can't help believing that they would have been married on a spot such as this, where they could look down at their village and out across his land. Only it would have been in the fall of the year after harvest when the leaves are bright and beautiful, and the weather cool and comfortable, of course."

"Of course," Huck agreed, reaching for her hand.

She turned to him, seeing in the strong lines of his jaw and the soft blue of his eyes the hero of her imagination, a man both sensitive and strong. Only he was more than that now. In these past several weeks, his constant courting and considerate ways had captured her heart, and for a fleeting moment she dared to dream of a day when she would become his forever at this very place, with friends and family close by and a view of unspeakable beauty beyond.

Gazing deep into Lavinia's eyes, Huck sensed new warmth in their brown depths, born of the soul within. How he yearned to ask for her hand, to make her his own. She was even dreaming aloud about a fall wedding from this very place! But he would not raise the matter of marriage now, for he had learned his lesson well on that day in May when the mushrooms and trilliums were in bloom. Only time would tell if a pig iron man from Wisconsin would do. More time must pass. He must be certain of the answer he would receive. Just as important, he must be certain that he had repaid his debt to his uncle, a debt that was shrinking but not yet paid in full.

Regardless, when he gazed down at Flora and Stubby, so peaceful and content, he couldn't help dreaming of the day when he and Lavinia would have children and pets of their own. Quietly, he asked, "Did Palemon and your namesake have young ones?"

Lavinia nodded. "They 'reared a numerous offspring, lovely like themselves, and good, the grace of all the country round,' according to the poem."

"Then they must have had children much like Flora, I would assume."

Lavinia smiled. "I would assume."

Flora stirred and yawned. "Are you talking to me?"

Huck said, "No, but it's good you're awake. It's time we head home before the sun disappears altogether."

Lavinia took one last look at the fiery half-circle that had transformed blue waters to orange, then rose and started down the trail, her feet carrying her toward home while her thoughts and dreams remained on the view she left behind.

Flora and Stubby preceded her, and hadn't gone far when the puppy sat down. Flora tugged gently on his leash, her frustration reflected in her voice.

"Come on, Stubby! We've got to go home. It's getting dark!"

Huck bent down and lifted the mongrel into his arms. "Stubby's too tuckered out to walk home."

Lavinia said, "He's had a big day, moving to our place from the O'Connells'."

Huck said, "Flora, when you get home, be sure to give him some food and water, then let him get some sleep."

Flora asked, "What if he won't go to sleep? What if he's like Cubby and cries all night?"

Lavinia sighed. "I hope he's too tired for that, but if he does, you'll just have to sleep on the floor beside his crate. You certainly don't want him running off in the middle of the night the way Cubby did."

Flora nodded and yawned, and Lavinia could see that

her little sister was almost as tired as her new puppy. Even so, she managed to keep the pace toward home.

They were nearing the heart of town when a familiar voice called out.

"Huck! Lavinia!"

It was Big Billy Bassett. He came toward them from the direction of the shanty village, his bulky frame moving faster than Lavinia had ever seen before. She wondered what had sparked the fire of urgency beneath his feet, and prayed nothing was amiss for the big fellow.

Chapter 13

Big Billy drew near, a broad smile lighting his face, and pure excitement in his voice.

"Good news! Moira and I are to be married!"

Huck set Stubby down and slapped Billy on the back. "That's great news, friend!"

Lavinia extended her congratulations, asking, "When is the wedding?"

"In one month. You're both invited."

Huck said, "I wouldn't miss it!"

Billy laughed. "Good thing. I need you for a witness!" He stepped off in the direction of the hotel. "Got to go tell the other fellows. See you later!"

Huck nodded. Picking up the puppy again, he said, "What do you know, Stubby? Billy and Moira are going to be wed!" To Lavinia, he said, "I'm really glad for Billy's sake that the wedding is only four weeks away. For the last two months he's talked of nothing but Moira!"

Flora slipped her hand into Lavinia's as they started toward home again. "Does that mean Alice and Grace are getting a new uncle?"

"Yes, Flora," she said absently, still absorbing the fact of Billy's announcement. While the news of the event began to settle in her mind, an unfamiliar feeling rose deep within. All the way home she pondered this emotion that seemed to include a pinch each of jealousy, longing, desire, and fear all stirred together in the soup pot of her soul.

At the front door, Huck put Stubby down and handed his leash to Flora, saying, "Do you remember what I told you?"

Flora nodded. "Give Stubby some food and water, then let him get some sleep."

"That's right! Good night, Flora!"

"Good night!" She led her puppy inside.

Huck turned to Lavinia, taking her hands in his. "I should get back to the hotel. Billy's probably wearing out the patience of the other fellows with his talk of Moira and their wedding." He paused to gaze into Lavinia's eyes, seeing a depth and mystery in their brown hue that he'd never noticed before. "Are you all right? You've been mighty quiet for the last several minutes."

"I'm fine," she assured him, but her smile was less than convincing. "I've got a lot on my mind with Flora's new puppy and . . . "

Lavinia paused. Unwilling to speak of the strange feelings within, she simply concluded, "I'd better go and help Flora with Stubby."

"Good night, and sweet dreams, if Stubby will allow it!" With a squeeze of her hands, he released her and headed off at a brisk pace.

Once Stubby had been tended to and put in his crate for the night, it didn't take long for his whining to begin. With little hope of sleep, Lavinia lay between the sheets mulling over the news Big Billy had shared, and sorting out the strange feelings it had stirred within. This evening, sitting on the bluff with Huck and envisioning a wedding there, brought both longing and fear to her heart. While she longed to live out her dream of nuptials in a place of storybook splendor, she could not completely quiet her fear of commitment to a future in a pig iron town. As her desire to be with Huck had increased, this voice of fear had grown weaker, but it still maintained a peppery persistence. At the same time, counteracting it was the sweet siren of jealousy, its sugary song saying that if Moira and Billy could take their wedding vows, then why not she and Huck?

While jealousy and fear, longing and desire quietly simmered, Lavinia began to take an assessment of herself. She was almost seventeen, the age her mother was when she had married, but Lavinia wasn't nearly ready for the many practical responsibilities marriage entailed, especially in the kitchen. She had helped her mother many a time to prepare dinners and desserts, to clean up and tend the stove, and she had become a master at the art of biscuit baking, but she had never taken responsibility from beginning to end for a complete dinner. With her mother and grandmother doing battle there three times a day since the tutoring sessions for the immigrant scholars had recessed, she had made a point to avoid that part of the house when meals were being prepared. Now, she wanted and *needed* to spend time learning all she could from the two good cooks in her family. But the kitchen that had already proven too small for the two eldest women of the family would certainly not hold three. Silently, she prayed.

Lord, I need Your help. How can I learn to cook when our kitchen is already crowded with good cooks and tart tongues?

While she pondered her problem to the tune of Stubby's whining, an idea came to her, an idea that held promise for improving her cooking skills, and family relations, too. She waited until she and Flora had washed and put away the breakfast dishes, Toby had gone to work at the hotel, and her sister had taken Stubby out back to play with the new chew toy Grandma had made. Taking a deep breath,

Lavinia mentally reviewed the words she needed to say, then invited her mother and grandmother into the parlor for a chat. When they had made themselves comfortable, Grandma in the straight chair and her mother on the sofa, Lavinia sat across from them.

"Mama, Grandma," she began, making certain to put on a smile, "if there's one thing I have noticed about the two of you, it's the fact that you are both wonderful cooks. In fact, more than anything, I wish I knew how to cook as well as you!"

Grandma waved her concern aside. "You will, child, you will, when you've cooked as long as we have."

Mary added, "And when you've made as many mistakes as I have, you learn to be a good cook."

Lavinia said, "But, if each of you would spend some time teaching me your ways in the kitchen *now*, then I won't have to make mistakes *later*."

Mary asked, "Why are you so interested in cooking, all of a sudden?" Before Lavinia could answer, her mother continued. "It's Huck, isn't it? You want him to know that you can do more in the kitchen than bake flaky biscuits."

Lavinia said, "You've always claimed that a woman who could bake a good taffy tart would have a husband with a happy heart."

Grandma said, "I made up that saying when your mother was your age, and very interested in the attention your father was paying her."

Mary chuckled. "I was far more interested in spending time with Angus than in cooking or baking. But Mother managed to teach me how to bake the tarts, and on the very night that your father first tasted them—"

Lavinia finished for her. "He proposed marriage. I love that story. Now, I need to know how to bake the tarts and do all the other things you and Grandma do in the kitchen. I have this idea . . . "

Lavinia suggested that while school was in summer recess, she could work in the kitchen with her mother on Mondays, Wednesdays, and Fridays, and with her grandmother on Tuesdays, Thursdays, and Saturdays. On Sundays, she would do all the cooking by herself.

"This arrangement offers wonderful benefits," Lavinia pointed out. "You'll both have more time for the things you enjoy—sewing, fancywork, reading." Her focus on her mother, she added, "Or helping Flora to train and walk Stubby. What do you think of my idea, Mama? Are you and Grandma willing to teach me?"

Mary said, "There's no better student than an eager one."

Grandma nodded. "I'm honored that you asked, child. Of course I'll help you."

"Thank you, both!" She gave each of them a hug, and a kiss on the cheek. Then she turned to her mother. "Since today is Thursday, you can leave all the kitchen chores to Grandma and me." To her grandmother, she said, "What are we cooking for dinner today?"

"I had in mind a recipe my own mother often made about this time of the week when the Sunday roast was long gone and the Sabbath still three days off . . . "

Two weeks and two days later, as Lavinia lay in bed too hot to sleep on a Saturday night, she couldn't help mentally planning the meal she was to prepare all by herself for Sunday dinner. She would roast a chicken that would be as tender and delectable as the ones her grandma made, and she would bake taffy tarts as flaky and scrumptious as her mother's. And Huck would be there to taste them.

With the furnace in full operation on Sunday as on the other six days of the week, he would have only an hour for the midday meal, but it would be opportunity enough to prove her cooking skills. She longed to hear the compliments her mother and grandmother often earned for their efforts in the kitchen. But she wondered whether the food on the dinner plates would even warrant comment compared with the subject on everyone's mind—Billy and Moira's wedding.

On the very day after their betrothal, a stream of news began to flow that never let up. Alice O'Connell had been the first to report, giving details of the bridal gown.

"Aunt Moira ordered yards and yards of blue silk taffeta for her new dress. It's going to have lots of pleats and bows, and a ruffled overskirt! Mama's going to help her sew it."

Soon after, Huck reported that, "Billy and Moira have arranged for the ceremony to take place at six o'clock on Saturday, the fifteenth of next month. It will be held outdoors in front of the hotel if the weather is good, inside if it's not. Afterwards, there's going to be a reception with food and music and dancing and everyone's invited."

Many more details had followed, including progress on the dress and plans for the food and beverages that the ladies of the immigrant community would provide. And just last night Lavinia's father had said, "Billy and Moira will be living in one of the new cabins going up at the shanty village. It will be modest, but at least they won't have to start out sharing Paddy's place!"

Lavinia had never looked kindly on the cabins at the shanty village, but now they took on the romantic lure of a cottage for newlyweds, cozy and private. She could even see herself keeping house in such a place if she had a good cook stove, not just the open hearth common to many.

With dreamy thoughts of her own future, she drifted into semi-sleep, recalling the letter she had received a couple of days ago from her Aunt Everilda in Canada. She had renewed her invitation for Lavinia to come live with her when she turned seventeen. She had described in rich detail the life Lavinia would lead, attending services in the most prestigious church in town and going out to the social events held by the finest families of the county. She had even mentioned several eligible young men as potential suitors. But the idea of returning to Canada had lost its appeal, Lavinia realized. Her heart belonged to Huck, if not to Fayette.

That happy thought in mind, she fell into a sound sleep, waking early to cook her father's breakfast and see him off to work. When the entire family had been fed, she put her hand to the task of baking tarts. Her mother had taught her the secret to flaky tart crust, and she followed the instructions diligently, rolling out the dough and carefully fitting it into the tart pans. Then she prepared the taffy filling of sugar, a smidgen of molasses, a pinch of salt, two beaten eggs, and a piece of butter the size of a walnut. When she had poured it into the tart crusts and had set them in the oven to bake, she went in search of a bird to roast.

She had never slaughtered a chicken herself, but had watched her mother and grandmother many a time. Today, she would pick out and prepare a bird without their help. She looked for a bird that would make a nice, plump roaster and found an older hen from last year's stock that would suit the purpose. She thought it strange that the bird hadn't found its way into the roasting pan before now and concluded that her mother and grandmother had simply overlooked it.

The hen was easy to catch, but feisty when she began tying rope to each of its feet. After a few nasty pecks, she had accomplished her mission and proceeded to hang the bird from a tree branch at the back edge of the yard. Sharp knife in hand, she drew a deep breath. Then she swiftly slit its throat just behind the lower beak and dashed toward the house. While the bird flapped its last, she filled a bucket with hot water from the boiler on the stove. Then she untied the hen and swished it in the water for a minute or two until the feathers came off in sheets, starting with the tail and wings.

Pausing in her chicken preparation to check on her tarts, she saw that the crust had turned golden brown and the filling had set, so she removed them from the oven and put them on the counter to cool. Drawing a deep breath of their delicious aroma, she returned to the less appetizing chore of cleaning the chicken.

Ridding the bird of its unusable parts was the task she liked least, but she proceeded, breathing through her mouth to avoid the smell. After removing the feet, head, and the end of the neck, she got rid of the oil gland at the base of the tail. Then she tackled the innards, saving the giblets for gravy. In the kitchen, she prepared stuffing of cubed dried bread, butter, onion, and herbs and seasonings according to her grandmother's method. When she had filled the cavity, tied the feet together, tucked the wings behind the back, and basted with melted herb butter, she set the bird in the roaster and slid the pan into the oven, anticipating the delicious and tender chicken that would result at dinnertime.

For the next couple of hours, she joined her mother, grandmother, and sister in Grandma's room for scripture reading and prayer, excusing herself at various times to add wood to the kitchen stove and baste the chicken. The aroma of the roasting bird drifted in, prompting Grandma to say, "If that bird tastes half as good as it smells, we'll be dining better than the Queen of England today!"

"Thanks, Grandma," Lavinia replied modestly. "I hope you're right."

When mealtime was an hour away, Lavinia closed her Bible, saying, "I'd better pare the potatoes and set the dining table. I wouldn't want dinner to be late."

Mary said, "Your sister and I will set the table for you. You have enough to do in the kitchen."

"Thanks, Mama, Flora!"

Lavinia put a stack of dinner plates and the platter in the warming oven, then she set the giblets to simmering. Next, she pared and quartered the potatoes and covered them with water and put them on the stove to cook. She sharpened the carving knife, then washed the raspberries she had bought for six cents a quart from the Indians who had paddled into the harbor to sell them yesterday. Dividing the berries into small serving dishes, she drizzled honey over top, then put one dish at each place on the dining table.

Hot from her efforts in the kitchen, Lavinia stepped out back to pump cold water from the well and splash it on her face. Then she went up to her room to take off the old gray dress she had worn for slaughtering the chicken, and put on her good blue dress. Back in the kitchen, she whipped some heavy cream to garnish the taffy tarts and returned it to the icebox.

Now, with a quarter hour to go before the dinner whistle would blow, the moment of reckoning had come. With hot pads in hand, Lavinia removed the roasting pan from the oven and lifted off the lid. The bird was golden brown, the beautiful and glorious color that had always given her grandmother's roasters such appeal when they had arrived at the dining table for carving. Hopes high, Lavinia tested the leg joint for doneness, but it was not about to separate easily. Keen disappointment set in. With the bird not yet done, she couldn't make the gravy. Basting the chicken one last time, she returned the roasting pan to the oven, hoping the bird would be fully cooked but not too brown by the time the furnace whistle blew.

Turning her attention to the potatoes, she mashed them with butter, cream, and seasonings. She was putting them into a serving dish when the furnace whistle sounded.

A moment later her mother came to the kitchen door. "Huck and your father will be here any minute. Do you need help?" Before Lavinia could answer, Mary asked with alarm, "Haven't you taken the chicken out of the oven yet?"

Her nerves on edge, Lavinia replied, "I checked it fifteen minutes ago, but it wasn't quite done."

Mary headed for the stove. "Surely it's done now. I'll put it on the platter for you."

"Let me do it, Mama," Lavinia insisted, setting the potatoes in the warming oven and removing the platter.

Mary watched closely as Lavinia uncovered the roaster. "That's a large bird, but it has a nice, brown color." She tested the leg joint. "It's done. Would you like me to make the gravy?"

Lavinia shook her head. "Would you please chop the giblets, then take the stuffing out of the bird?"

While her mother did as asked, Lavinia put the chicken on the platter and set about making gravy according to the method her grandmother had taught her. She was pouring it into the gravy boat when she heard the creak of the pump handle out back and knew that her father and Huck were washing up for dinner.

Mary patted Lavinia on the shoulder. "Your dinner is

ready right on time!"

Lavinia stirred giblets into the gravy and handed the boat to her mother. "If you'll take this to the table, I'll bring out the chicken and the dishes in the warming oven."

She set a stack of dinner plates at her father's place, and the potatoes and stuffing nearby, then returned to the kitchen one last time. When Huck and the family had gathered around the table—all but Toby who was working at the hotel—Lavinia emerged from the kitchen carrying the golden brown bird, plump and delectable-looking with an aroma that would pique the appetite of the most finicky eater.

Huck smiled broadly. "Lavinia, your chicken looks and smells wonderful!"

Angus said, "So it does! Let's be seated!"

Huck held Lavinia's chair for her, then her father commenced the carving of the bird and the serving of stuffing and potatoes. When everyone had a full plate, Angus asked a blessing.

"We thank Thee, Lord, for the bountiful gifts of this day—good friends, good food, good weather, and good pig iron, in Jesus' name, Amen." He helped himself to the gravy and passed it on.

Lavinia ladled gravy over her meat and potatoes, then cut into her portion of chicken breast with the side of her fork. To her dismay, the job called for her dinner knife and a dedicated effort to separate a bite-size piece. In her mouth, the breast meat tasted fine, but required a great amount of chewing. There was no getting around the fact that the chicken was *tough!*

Apprehension set in. She consoled herself with the fact that Huck was eating dark meat, a thigh. Perhaps it was more tender than the white meat. He took his first bite and smiled, then chewed.

164

Flora wasted no time picking up her drumstick and biting off a piece. After a little chewing, she started to talk. "This chicken is awfully—ouch!" She turned to Grandma. "You just kicked me! Why did you kick me?"

"Don't talk with food in your mouth, Flora!" To Lavinia, Grandma said, "This chicken is awfully tasty!"

Mary nodded, adding, "And the potatoes are creamy and smooth!"

Angus said, "The stuffing is excellent, Lavinia! That's always my favorite part of the meal."

Huck had put aside his fork and knife to tuck his spoon into the fresh raspberries. "Mmm. Is that honey I taste? Delicious!"

Her cheeks burning, her stomach sour, Lavinia exclaimed, "The truth is, this chicken is *tough!*" Setting down her fork and knife with a clank, she excused herself and dashed out the back door.

Chapter

14

So embarrassed was Lavinia for serving tough chicken to Huck and her family that she kept right on going until she'd reached the back of the yard where Stubby was tied to a maple tree. He jumped with joy to see her.

She knelt beside him and he licked the tears from her cheeks. Enfolding him in her arms, she buried her face in his shiny red coat, telling him, "You're the only one who doesn't mind that my chicken is tough!"

Huck's voice sounded from behind. "That's not exactly true."

Lavinia gazed up at him, then turned away, humiliation keen.

Huck sat down beside her. "I'm sorry you're so upset over the chicken, Lavinia, but you needn't be. Even the best of cooks runs into a tough bird once in a while."

More tears dampened her cheeks. "I'm sorry, Huck," she mumbled, her throat tight with disappointment. "I wanted so badly for everything to be perfect for you today!"

Huck placed his arm about her waist and drew her to him, letting her sob against his shoulder while Stubby snuggled close. When an interval had passed and her tears had dried, Huck said, "Let's go back inside. I understand that you've planned a special dessert."

Suddenly, she remembered. "The tarts!"

Huck whisked her to her feet, then walked her to the house, his arm firmly wrapped about her waist.

When they reached the dining room, Lavinia saw that the table had already been cleared and everyone sat waiting.

Flora asked, "May I help you serve the tarts now, Livvy?"

She smiled. "Please do, Flora!"

Within moments, a taffy tart topped with a generous dollop of whipped cream had arrived at each place.

Angus wasted no time tasting his. "Delicious, Lavinia! Crusty on the top, soft and sugary inside—just like your mother's!"

Mary nodded. "Maybe better. I think your crust is more tender."

Lavinia beamed. "Thank you, Papa, Mama!"

Similar comments were forthcoming from Flora and Grandma, but Huck said nothing. He had polished off all but his last bite before he offered an opinion. "I don't mean to be tardy with my compliment," he began.

Lavinia laughed. "Tardy, or 'tarty'?"

He chuckled. "I mean, your taffy tart is so good, I almost couldn't stop eating it to tell you!" He popped the last morsel into his mouth.

Flora pinned a worried look on Huck. "You're not going to eat all the leftover tarts the way Big Toby did, are you?"

Huck laughed. "No, but I'm sorely tempted!"

Mary spoke thoughtfully. "I wonder whatever became of Big Toby. He's been gone more than two weeks now."

Grandma said, "I think he's home with his Aunt Edna, safe and sound."

Flora frowned. "I hope you're wrong! She was mean to him!"

Angus put up a quieting hand. "We don't know everything about Big Toby and his aunt, or how that story ends, but there's a story I *do* know. It's about the first time I tasted a taffy tart and I'm going to tell it to Huck now." He focused on the young man. "I was very fond of Mary when she and I were the same age as Lavinia and you are right now."

When he paused to smile reflectively, Mary said, "Back then, I didn't know nearly as much as Lavinia does about cooking, nor did I want to."

Angus told Huck, "I didn't know Mary couldn't cook. I only knew that I wanted to spend as much time with her as I could."

Grandma said, "And Mary thought of nothing but Angus. When she'd help me in the kitchen she was so distracted I could hardly get any work out of her at all!"

Angus continued. "But like I said, I didn't know that. In fact, I didn't know for certain how Mary felt about me. I only knew that our time together was like magic for me, and I could hardly bear to leave her at the end of the evening."

Mary said, "Of course, I had no idea how strongly Angus felt about me. But I knew that I must have him for my husband one day, and I told Mama so."

Grandma said, "That's when I told Mary that the way to win Angus's affections was to learn how to cook for him."

Mary chuckled. "I didn't have a heart for cooking. I only had a heart for Angus. He had captured it completely!"

Flora said, "So Grandma made up a little saying. 'A woman who can bake a good taffy tart will have a husband with a happy heart!'"

Lavinia said, "That's when Mama first learned to bake taffy tarts."

Mary said, "It wasn't easy. Mama helped me one day and that evening when Angus came to call, I served him a taffy tart."

Angus said, "One bite, and I knew I must make Mary my wife! I was so eager to have her promised to me that when I finished the tart, I dropped to my knee, and said, 'Mary, will you bake taffy tarts for me for the rest of our lives—if your folks will give their blessing, that is?'"

Mary said, "Of course, I agreed. My folks gave us their blessing, and we were married soon after."

Angus said, "Mary was seventeen." He paused, adding, "Lavinia will soon be seventeen."

Lavinia's cheeks burned, but before she could halt further discussion on the topic, Grandma told Huck, "Her birthday is a week from next Saturday."

And Flora asked, "You're coming for dinner, aren't you, Huck? We always have roast beef on Livvy's birthday, and ginger cake. They're her favorites."

Huck hesitated, hoping to hear an invitation from Lavinia herself.

Mary said, "Do come, Huck. Your company is always welcome."

Lavinia said, "I'll be expecting you."

Huck smiled. "Then, I'll be here!"

Several days later

Heat from the oven along with the moist warmth of the August morning made Lavinia damp with perspiration as she measured the flour, and the fragrant ginger, cloves, and cinnamon for the molasses cake her mother was teaching her to bake. She was passing the dry ingredients through a sifter when a knock sounded on the front door.

Mary set aside the bowl in which she had measured the butter with the sugar. "It's got to be the O'Connell twins. They show up nearly every day at this time."

Lavinia could hear her mother calling Flora down from the bedroom where she went daily to play with the fancy doll and rocking chair she had received for her birthday a few weeks earlier. She heard, too, the scamper of her sister's feet and those of Stubby racing down the stairs. Her mother had returned to the kitchen to cream the butter and sugar when Flora burst in, full of excitement.

"Alice and Grace are getting fancy new dresses to wear at Moira's wedding! Their mama is making them right now out of taffeta, and lace, and—may I go to O'Connells' and see, Mama?"

"You may, but you must be home in time for dinner. Don't forget—"

"I will! I promise!"

In a flash, the little girl was gone.

Mary smiled and shook her head. "I was going to remind her to tie Stubby outside. Maybe she took him along."

Lavinia was barely listening, her focus on the ingredients she had measured and sifted. "Mama, did you say a pinch of ginger, or two pinches?"

"Two of ginger, one each of cloves and cinnamon."

"Good! That's what I put in. The dry ingredients are measured and sifted three times."

Mary said, "While I finish creaming the butter and sugar, you may beat two eggs, then measure out a teacup of molasses and a coffee cup of milk mixed with three pinches of soda."

Lavinia followed her mother's instructions, trying to commit each ingredient to memory as she worked, repeating the list again and again out loud until her mother began to laugh. "I do believe you'll make a song of this recipe if you repeat it a few more times."

"To the tune of *Oh, Susanna*, don't you think?" Lavinia replied, putting the ingredients to the folk melody with moderate success.

Minutes later, her mother poured the batter into a cake pan and slipped it into the oven. "While that's baking, we'd best get started on the scalloped potatoes and ham. We'll need half a dozen potatoes from the bin. Why don't you start peeling while I dice the ham."

Lavinia set to work. She had peeled one potato and was starting on the second when Stubby bounded into the kitchen and nearly snatched the ham from the counter.

"Stubby, down!" Mary commanded, pushing him away.

He sat and stared up at her, tail wagging ever so slightly.

Mary sighed. "I thought Flora took you with her. Evidently, I was wrong. I'll have to have a talk with her when she comes home."

Lavinia said, "I'll tie Stubby outside." Taking a morsel of ham in one hand, and Stubby by the collar with the other, she easily led him to the tree in back where she tied him securely. When she had taken him a bowl of water and another of table scraps, she returned to her kitchen chores. Half an hour later, the molasses cake came out of the oven and the scalloped potatoes and ham went in, baking to perfection by the time the dinner whistle blew.

Flora arrived home a couple of minutes later, bursting into the kitchen with excitement. "Look at the taffeta and lace for Alice's and Grace's dresses!" She held up small swatches of the pale blue fabric and the ecru lace.

Lavinia paused to inspect. "Aren't they fancy! The

twins will look as beautiful as their aunt!"

Mary said, "Lovely, indeed! Now, go and wash. Dinner's ready. Your father will soon be here."

"Yes, Mama," Flora replied, skipping into her grandmother's room to show the swatches there before washing at the pump out back.

Lavinia turned to her mother. "I thought you were going to have a talk with her about Stubby."

Mary nodded. "I'll do it after dinner, when your father's gone back to work. I couldn't bring myself to spoil her excitement. Besides, a scolding is no appetizer for the fine meal we're about to put on the table."

Minutes later, Lavinia helped her mother serve the scalloped potatoes and ham, and the molasses cake to high compliments from her father and grandmother. Conversation was exceptionally convivial, with Flora excited about the O'Connell girls' dresses, Angus pleased with production at the furnace, and Grandma delighted with the quilt square she had completed for the quilt the ladies in the community were making for Moira's wedding. Lavinia took to heart her mother's lesson about not ruining a cheerful mood and tasty meal with a scolding that could wait.

Dinner over, she began stacking dirty dishes while her father headed back to the furnace, Grandma retired to her room, and Flora bounded up the stairs to her room. Lavinia was carrying a pile of plates to the kitchen where her mother was preparing a pan of dishwater when a blood-curdling scream from the room above penetrated down through the floorboards.

"Flora?" Lavinia cried, nearly dropping the plates as panic set in.

Her mother ran past her en route to the stairs, narrowly avoiding a collision with her.

Setting the china on the kitchen table, Lavinia dashed after her mother, heart pounding.

Chapter

15

Lavinia's jaw went slack at the sight that met her when she reached the bedroom door. Scraps of pink silk were everywhere, the remains of Flora's birthday doll's dress. And strewn across the floor with them were patches of muslin from the body and tufts of cotton batting from the stuffing that had filled arms, legs, and torso. Flora wailed inconsolably despite her mother's earnest efforts to calm her.

Lavinia stooped to pick up a patch of muslin containing the heart she had embroidered on the doll's chest. Beside it were the remains of its head. Yellow yarn hair, now chewed and tangled, framed a face pitted with teeth marks. Nearby, the chair her father, brother, and Huck had made was missing the tip of the left rocker, gnawed off by a mischievous pup. Unattended, Stubby had wreaked havoc until his appetite had overruled his fascination with forbidden objects and the aroma of tasty ham had drawn him to the kitchen.

Laying the muslin remnant on the chair, Lavinia sat beside Flora on her bed where her mother was trying unsuccessfully to comfort her.

"I hate Stubby! I *hate* him!" Flora insisted between sobs.

Mary spoke sympathetically. "I'm sorry this happened, dear. I know how much you loved your new dolly and her chair. I wish I could make things better."

Lavinia took her sister's hand in her own. "Maybe we can make you a new dolly, Flora. She wouldn't be exactly like the last one, but—"

"I don't want a new dolly! I want my birthday doll back again!" Flora insisted, breaking down in a new round of sobs.

Unable to quiet her distraught sister, Lavinia asked God to give comfort to Flora, then began cleaning up the mess, gathering it in a pillowcase and carrying it downstairs. She was about to toss a handful of the shredded fabric into the kitchen stove when Grandma came to the door.

"What's the matter with Flora? And what are you putting in the stove?" She came closer. "Isn't that the pink silk I used for Flora's doll dress?"

Lavinia nodded, showing her the contents of the pillowcase. "Stubby's doing."

Grandma clucked her tongue and retreated to her room.

Disposing of the last of the doll, Lavinia returned to the kitchen chores. While her mother remained upstairs by Flora's side, she tidied dining room and kitchen, silently asking God how a new doll might be fashioned that would be pleasing to Flora. By the time she had put away the clean dishes, an idea had come to her. With a brief explanation to her grandmother, she stepped out on her errand of sisterly love, returning half an hour later with the necessary provisions in hand. Hearing voices in the back room, she hastened there to find her mother and grandmother in conversation. Her grandmother was speaking.

"I knew it would be just a matter of time before that pup ruined your nicest things. I told you that from the start, but as usual, you were too independent-minded to listen."

Mary sighed. "Such pronouncements are of no help

right now. Can't you understand that Flora is heartbroken?"

"I can, just as she was heartbroken when Cubby died!" Grandma replied. "I will do my part to replace the doll. But the whole problem could have been avoided if you'd followed my advice and stayed clear of the pup in the first place."

"Well, we didn't!" Mary sprang to her feet. "The pup's part of the family, and we're going to make the best of it, the same as when I was a child and we had that spaniel!" She headed out back, straight for the shade tree where Stubby lay.

Lavinia silently retreated from the room and climbed the stairs. Even before she reached the bedroom she could hear the muffled sobs of her sister. She sat beside her and caressed her shoulder. "Look at what I have here, Flora! Something you're going to like very much!" She lay the brown paper package beside her sister.

"I don't want it," Flora muttered, "all I want is my dolly."

"And you'll have her back looking better than ever," Lavinia promised, opening the package to reveal the piece of blue taffeta and length of lace the O'Connells had given her, and the muslin and cotton batting she had purchased at the company store.

Flora sat up and spread the taffeta across her lap. Almost smiling, she asked, "How long do you suppose it will take to make another dolly?"

Lavinia shrugged. "The sooner you take these things to Grandma and ask for her help, the sooner she can get started."

Without another word, Flora gathered up the items and carried them to her grandmother.

Lavinia quietly thanked God for answered prayer.

Two days later, after Flora had gone to the O'Connells' to play, Lavinia heard Stubby whining out back and realized her sister had left him tied to the tree with no food or water. She filled his bowls and carried them to him, watching while he eagerly devoured their contents. When he had finished, he nudged her hand, begging for affection. Eager for a break from her kitchen chores on this hot summer day, Lavinia sat down beside him and stroked his shiny red coat and rubbed his belly. She was troubled by the knowledge that since the incident with the doll, she had not seen Flora giving even a shred of affection to the pup. She had even declined to walk him in the evenings, leaving her and Huck to tend to the chore without her. When Lavinia rose to return to her kitchen chores, Stubby whined, begging her to stay. She gave him one last scratch behind the ears and headed inside, pondering how to reconcile dog and child.

Later that afternoon, when Flora returned from visiting her friends, Lavinia said, "Stubby missed you. Why don't you go out back and sit with him for a while?"

"Not now," Flora replied, dashing up the stairs.

Lavinia followed, and invited her sister to sit beside her on the bed, then put her arm around the child. "I know you're upset over what Stubby did the other day, but don't you think it's time to put your anger aside?"

"No! I hate him! I wish Mama would just send him away!" she insisted with a pout.

"Do you really think that would be the right thing to do?" Lavinia asked gently. When a quiet moment lapsed, she added, "I know Stubby isn't perfect, but he's been a loyal, affectionate friend, and he desperately needs you to be the same. How would you feel if you were in his place, and the one person you cared for most would have nothing more to do with you?"

Flora stared silently at the floor.

Making one last point, Lavinia said, "A month ago, we made Stubby a member of this family. He deserves better from you."

Lavinia returned to the kitchen where she was helping her mother with the supper preparations when Flora came in. "Mama, I know it's near suppertime, but I'm awfully hungry. May I have a cookie, please? I *promise* I'll eat everything on my plate."

Mary hesitated, then granted her request. The little girl headed for Grandma's room, not pausing to chat but continuing out the back door.

Curious, Lavinia followed, watching from inside while Flora went straight for Stubby. Commanding the dog to sit, she fed him the entire cookie, one morsel at a time, and when it was gone, she sat down beside him, wrapping her arms around him while Stubby washed her face with kisses.

With a silent prayer of thanks, Lavinia returned to the kitchen, a sense of satisfaction settling over her.

The following day dawned loud and dark when a thunderstorm blew in across the bay, nearly drowning out the sound of the morning whistle. Lavinia had risen early to cook breakfast for her father, only to be told by her mother and grandmother to go back to bed and do no work on this, her seventeenth birthday, but she was too excited to sleep. Tonight, Huck would come for her birthday supper, and he had already told her he had a very important question to ask. In her mind, she could see him on bended knee and feel the warmth of his hand enfolding hers. But at the very moment he began to speak, a clap of thunder jolted her from her reverie.

Impatient for the day to begin, she rose and dressed and headed for the dining room where her grandmother presented her with a heart-shaped pancake. Breakfast over, she sat in her grandmother's rocker and sewed seams for the dress for Flora's new doll while her mother and grandmother began work on the ginger cake that would be served for her birthday supper.

With the storm continuing to rumble, she worked tiny stitches in the delicate blue taffeta, the same fabric that Alice and Grace would wear at Moira and Billy's wedding a week from today. Lavinia couldn't help envying the couple who would be the first to wed in the town of Fayette. Having spent a month in the kitchen learning everything a good cook would need to know, she now felt fully confident to meet the demands of a new bride. She had even mastered the task of choosing a chicken of the proper age for roasting, avoiding tough, old birds that were good only for stewing.

Such were the thoughts that filled her mind as her fingers worked with needle and thread. By mid-morning she had finished the seams of the doll dress and began applying the lace to the hem. She had taken but a few stitches when the furnace whistle began to blow, not the calm blast signaling dinner or a change of shifts, but frantic repeated blasts. From the kitchen came her mother's panicky words.

"There's trouble at the furnace! I've got to go and see if Angus is all right!"

"I'm coming with you, Mama!" Lavinia cried, concern for her father and Huck setting her in motion.

Grabbing umbrellas from the stand, they charged out the front door together. With no regard for puddles, Lavinia lifted her skirt and petticoat and began to run down the hill toward town, praying for God's help as she went. A crowd had gathered at the harbor side of the furnace where pig iron bars were stockpiled several layers high for shipment. Pressing through the knot of sooty, smelly men, she saw her father, Huck, and Paddy O'Connell carrying Big Billy Bassett away from a tumbled-down stack of iron pigs while the huge fellow by the name of Arthur Walters looked on.

Moira and Mrs. O'Connell arrived in time to see them lay Billy on a patch of grass outside the casting house. They rushed to Billy's side, obviously distraught.

Dr. Sloane hurried to the scene, setting his black bag aside to examine Billy's left leg.

Lavinia's mother joined her moments later, out of breath. "Thank the Lord . . . your father is all right. Do you know what happened?"

Lavinia shook her head.

Mr. De Longpre and Mr. Roempke, whose children had attended tutoring sessions, were standing nearby. Mr. De Longpre grumbled. "It's the fault of that Walters fellow."

Mr. Roempke nodded. "He may be stronger than all the rest, but he don't know diddle when it comes to stackin' pigs in a wheelbarrow."

Mr. De Longpre said, "It weren't no accident his load fell and landed on Billy's leg. He's had it in for Billy from the start—jealous that everybody likes him so well. Harrigan saw it coming and pushed his pal out of the way, or he'd have been hurt far worse. As it is, he'll be out of work for months—maybe forever."

Mary said, "Let's go home, Lavinia. There's nothing we can do here, and your sister and grandmother are waiting for news."

Lavinia hesitated. "I wish I could offer assistance or comfort or do *something* to help."

Mary shook her head. "Dr. Sloane is here. You'd only be in his way. Let's go." She nudged Lavinia toward home.

Casting a backward glance, Lavinia followed her mother, deeply troubled over Billy's injury. At home, when she tried to concentrate on her sewing, she couldn't get the accident out of her mind. The words of Mr. Roempke and Mr. De Longpre silently repeated over and over, and the vision of Billy lying helpless flashed before her repeatedly. Like molten iron from a furnace, fears flowed in, forcing all else from her mind. Her father's safety had been a constant concern for as long as Lavinia could remember. Now, she worried about Huck as well. And with suspicion over the Walters fellow rising, there was no telling what could happen next. In no time, all her reasons for hating this raw, unrefined village came flooding back, filling her with dread.

When the dinner whistle blew and her father didn't come home, she fretted even more, despite her mother's confidence that the accident had caused a delay. He walked through the door an hour late. Lavinia was the first to greet him, throwing her arms about him.

"I'm so glad you're home, Papa! I was worried!"

He kissed her cheek. "No need to worry about me, daughter. This is your day to celebrate! Happy Birthday!"

"Thank you, Papa." She hugged him once more before letting go.

Flora, Mary, and Grandma joined them, Mary asking, "How is Billy?"

He said, "I'll tell you over dinner. You saved some for me, I pray?"

Grandma said, "No one has eaten yet."

Flora said, "I'm starved!"

Angus smiled. "I'll go wash. Then, we'll sit down to

181

the table." Minutes later, when he had said grace and passed the pork chops and potatoes, he said, "Dr. Sloane expects Billy to recover completely from the accident in a month or two. By some miracle of the Almighty, no bones were broken, but his left leg was badly twisted, and it's severely bruised and swollen. He'll be off his feet for some time."

Lavinia said, "Are he and Moira still getting married next Saturday?"

Angus shook his head. "The wedding is postponed. I think that hurts Billy more than his leg!"

Mary said, "I heard talk from Mr. Roempke and Mr. De Longpre that perhaps that Walters fellow had purposely stacked his pigs so as to fall on Billy."

Angus grew thoughtful. "They told me their suspicions, and Huck spoke with me, too. In fact, that was most of the reason for my delay. The truth is, we can't say for a certainty that Walters hurt Billy on purpose. Now, enough about the accident, this is a day for joy and happiness! Lavinia is seventeen years old!"

She set her fork down, her food nearly untouched. "I don't feel very happy right now, or very hungry. May I please be excused?"

Angus grew solemn. "If you wish. Do you suppose your appetite will show up for the roast beef and ginger cake your mother and grandmother are planning for supper tonight?"

Lavinia replied with a shrug. Eager to be alone, she headed up the stairs, her grandmother's words floating up to her.

"Only time will tell. I remember Mary at her age, moody and unpredictable. One minute, she'd be laughing. Then, for no apparent reason, she'd turn sullen."

Alone in her room, Lavinia traveled hundreds of miles

in her thoughts and in her dreams without taking a single step. But whether awake or napping, she couldn't shake the vision of the accident that periodically came back to her unbidden.

The five o'clock whistle brought her instantly home to Fayette. A knock on the door and her mother's voice set her on her feet.

"Lavinia? Are you all right?"

She opened the door and forced a smile. The aroma of roast beef wafted in, but the thought of food only tightened the knot in her stomach. "I'm fine," she assured her mother, taking liberty with the truth.

"Good! Your father and Huck will be here any minute for supper."

"I'll be right there," she promised, taking time to smooth her dress and brush her hair before heading down the stairs. Shooed from the kitchen like an unwanted fly, she sat in her grandmother's room to wait while her father and Huck washed up at the pump. They came through the back door with smiles on their faces.

Her father kissed her on the cheek. "I hope you've found your appetite. Dinner smells mighty good." He headed for the kitchen.

Huck paused to gaze into her eyes, his own blue ones gleaming. "Happy Birthday, Lavinia!"

Again, she forced a smile. "Thank you, Huck."

Before either of them could say more, Grandma announced dinner.

Huck offered his arm. "May I?"

She nodded, allowing him to escort her to her place at the dining table where he held her chair, then sat beside her. Somehow, she managed to put on a pleasant face and eat reasonable portions of roast beef, baked potato, and corn, masking the disconsolate pain that throbbed with every beat of her heart.

When she had blown out the candle on the ginger cake, cut and served the pieces with generous portions of whipped cream, and found and given away the blessing coin, her mother said, "We all have a present for you after supper."

Her father said, "It was Huck's idea."

Flora said, "It's waiting for you in the parlor."

Grandma said, "It's so nice, I wish I'd had one like it at your age."

Her mother said, "So do I! But then, there'd have been no need for this one. We could have simply passed it down to Lavinia."

Flora said, "Can you guess what it is, Livvy?"

"I haven't any idea," she replied, fearing what it might be, and regretting the trouble they'd gone to. Regardless, minutes later they led her to the parlor where a large object draped with an old sheet stood in the center of the floor.

She was wondering how such a bulky item could have escaped her notice when her father said, "I'm glad you decided to take a nap this afternoon. I was afraid you'd catch us delivering your present and spoil the surprise."

Huck nudged her forward. "Go on, uncover it."

Tentatively, she stepped forward. Grasping the corner of the sheet, she gently pulled it off, little by little unveiling an oblong maple chest that had been varnished to a high gloss. In the center of the lid was carved a huge heart, leaving no doubt in her mind that this chest was meant to hold the linens that she would acquire for her wedding day.

Her mother said, "Huck and your father and brother made that chest for you. Inside are the gifts from Grandma and Flora and me."

Lavinia lifted the lid to discover a set of pillowcases finely embroidered with trilliums and a hot pad with a trillium appliqued onto the center in large, uneven stitches.

Flora said, "Mama and Grandma made the pillowcases and I made the hot pad all by myself!"

Lavinia gazed lovingly at the white blossom. "I'll treasure it always, Flora." Her throat tightening, she added, "And this chest. It will be my special keepsake forever." Fighting back tears, she lowered the lid and traced the deeply chiseled heart with her finger, wishing her own heart were not about to break.

Angus said, "I believe it's time for Stubby's walk. Mary, Flora, shall we go?"

Grandma said, "And I hear dirty dishes calling."

In an instant, Lavinia was alone with Huck.

He came close. Keenly aware that her emotions were on edge, he said quietly, "Come sit on the sofa."

His mellow voice was a balm to her soul, his hand at her elbow a comforting guide. But panic rose anew when, instead of sitting beside her, he knelt, taking her hands in both of his.

Huck gazed up into Lavinia's brown eyes. For a moment, he thought he saw a look of fright there. Then moisture welled up, softening her gaze, so he drew a breath to deliver the words he had rehearsed dozens of times over the last few days.

"Lavinia, I love you with all my heart. I want to be with you always, and forever. Will you do me the honor of becoming my bride? I'll have repaid my Uncle Sean by the end of the year. Then I'll be more than able to support you, the furnace going strong as it is."

A tear slid down her cheek, then another. But while her heart screamed yes, she forced her tongue to make a different reply.

"I'm sorry. I can't marry you. Not at the end of the year—not ever!"

Her terse words sliced him through and rendered him speechless. She withdrew to the window. Though her back was to him, he could see that she was wiping away more tears. But when she turned to him again, her cheeks were dry, her jaw set.

"I can't spend my life in this miserable town worrying every second of every day whether you'll come home to me on two feet, or be carried through the door, injured and helpless."

Suddenly, Huck understood. He started toward her. "Billy's accident has scared you silly. Don't let it, Lavinia! Don't let it ruin what we feel for one another!"

She put palms out. "I've made up my mind, Huck. I'll never marry a pig iron man. I don't want to see you again."

"But—"

"I'm leaving this place. I'm going to live with my Aunt Everilda. My decision is final."

He couldn't believe what he was hearing. Her statements stung him into silence. Anger burned within. Suddenly, words flowed forth, unstoppable as molten iron running onto the casting house floor.

"I'm sorry to hear that, Lavinia. You certainly had me fooled, baking your taffy tarts for me like you did. I can see now that as far as you're concerned, my love is like so much slag to be drained off and tossed away. Good bye, Lavinia, you needn't worry about me coming around here anymore!" He strode out the door with nary a backward glance.

Chapter 16

One week later

"It's not fair!" Flora hurled the accusation at Lavinia from outside their locked bedroom door. "I can't wait until you go to Canada! Then, I can come in the room anytime I want. It's not fair!" she repeated.

Lavinia lay on her bed, listening to Flora's footsteps retreating down the stairs. She didn't care if her little sister thought she was unfair by locking her out of their bedroom. She needed time alone. Since the day after she'd turned seventeen, she hadn't wanted to be with anyone, talk to anyone, or do anything.

Rising, she stood at the foot of her bed beside her trunk and lifted the lid, stared at the few items she hadn't unpacked when she'd arrived in Fayette last fall, and closed it again. Since her decision to return to Canada, she hadn't made the first move to pack her belongings. She couldn't envision herself on a boat actually leaving Snail-Shell Harbor. In a week's time, the only visions that had come to mind were those of Big Billy Bassett lying helpless after his accident, and Huck walking out of the parlor after she had turned down his proposal of marriage.

Despondency had moved in with a grip strong as iron, stealing her ambition and multiplying the hours of every day until each one seemed twice as long as before. Afternoons dragged by, seemingly endless, alone with her reflections and woes. Evenings were worse now that Huck was gone from her life. And she could not get out of the mud that had mired her in this hopeless melancholy.

She ate little at supper, and as soon as the dishes had been washed and put away she headed back upstairs. Two hours later, Flora knocked on the door.

"Livvy? Let me in. Mama says it's my bedtime."

Without a word, Lavinia unlocked the door, then lay down again.

Flora sat on her bed beside her.

Lavinia gazed up, grumbling. "I thought Mama sent you to bed. Why don't you get into your nightgown instead of just sitting there, staring at me?"

Flora chewed on her braid. "There's something I have to tell you."

"Then tell me," Lavinia said grumpily.

"Do you remember when I was mad at Stubby, because he ruined my doll and rocker?"

"What's that got to do with anything?" Lavinia asked.

"Well, Huck hasn't even done anything wrong, but you sent him away. How would you feel if you were in his place, and the one person you cared for most would have nothing more to do with you?"

"Go get ready for bed. You don't know what you're talking about," Lavinia said testily.

"Do, too!" Flora insisted. "A long time ago, Huck got to be just like a member of this family. He deserves better from you!" She got up and began dressing for bed.

Lavinia pondered Flora's words. A seven-year-old child couldn't possibly understand the problem. How dare she compare this situation to the one with Stubby? There just wasn't any similarity at all, was there?

The question was still lingering in Lavinia's mind when

Flora had finished putting on her nightgown and got into bed. Moments later, Lavinia heard Toby coming upstairs, evidently finished with his work at the hotel. But instead of going straight to his own room, he paused outside Lavinia and Flora's open door, speaking softly.

"Livvy, may I talk to you for a minute?"

She nodded, beckoning him to enter.

He came beside the bed where she lay. "I just wanted to tell you that I hope you don't move back to Canada."

Flora popped up. "*I* hope she *does!* You don't know what it's like, Toby, getting locked out of your room all the time."

Toby gave her a cross look. "Hush, Flora!" To Lavinia, he said, "She doesn't mean it."

"Do, too!" Flora insisted.

Ignoring his little sister, Toby told Lavinia, "It won't be the same here without you, I don't care what Flora says." He took a shuffling step toward the door.

Lavinia sat up. "Toby?"

He paused, his gaze meeting hers.

"I'll miss you, too."

He smiled briefly, then worry lines appeared between his brows. "Livvy, may I tell you something?"

She nodded, curious as to what could be troubling him.

"I think Huck's sick," he stated bluntly, then continued. "He hasn't had much appetite since you stopped seeing him, and he gives away his dessert to the other fellas that eat at the hotel. I just thought you ought to know." He hurried out of the room before she could reply.

She lay down, mulling over what Toby had said. His words were still on her mind when she drifted into a troubled sleep.

*   *   *

Lavinia picked at the ham her grandmother had served for supper. Of the five days that had passed since Flora's and Toby's discussions about Huck, each one had proved more miserable than the last. Lavinia's appetite was still gone, her ambition on extended leave, her outlook darker than storm clouds, and her ability to pray, nonexistent.

Her father spoke encouragingly. "Please try to eat, Lavinia, before you get any paler and thinner than you already are."

"I'm not hungry," she replied, setting down her fork.

Her mother said, "Maybe we should take you to Dr. Sloane. He probably has a tonic that would perk you up."

Grandma shook her head. "I doubt that a doctor or a tonic would help. What she needs is a visit from Huck!"

Flora said, "I think I should invite him to come to dinner."

"You'll do no such thing!" Lavinia insisted, pushing back from the table. On winged feet she fled to her room and locked the door. Lying on her bed, she heard the murmur of voices as the others finished supper and dessert, then the clanking of plates being cleared away. She was glad when no one called her down to wash dishes, but anxious when she heard the sound of her father's footsteps climbing the stairs.

He knocked on her door, then spoke quietly. "Lavinia? May I come in, please?"

She unlocked the door, then returned to her bed to sit.

He sat alongside her, taking her hand in his. "Lavinia, dear, you have me worried. I've never seen you so glum. Is there anything I can do to cheer you up?"

Lavinia treasured the secure feeling of his hand wrapped around hers. When she was a child, his touch alone had chased troubles away. But now that she was older, he would not be able to lift her spirits so easily.

She squeezed his hand and met his loving gaze. "There's nothing you can do, Papa, but thank you for asking."

He casually made his way toward the door, pausing beside her trunk. "I'll help you pack for your trip to Aunt Everilda's, if you like. Maybe we should do it tonight, right now."

"Not now, not tonight," she quickly replied.

"You *are* still planning to go to Canada, aren't you?"

She lowered her gaze.

After a moment's silence he said, "You may go to Canada or remain in Fayette, as you wish, but I'll not have you coming in here and locking out your little sister any more. Do you understand?"

Gaze fixed on the floor, she replied meekly, "Yes, Papa."

"Good!" After a thoughtful moment, he continued. "Now, I wish I could find a way to get Huck into better humor at work. Since the day after your birthday, he's been so cantankerous all the fellows are angry with him. You wouldn't have any ideas, would you?"

Lavinia shook her head.

"Too bad. Maybe I'll just have to let him go, then."

"You can't do that!" Lavinia argued, her focus squarely on her father.

"Sure I can. I'm his boss. Besides, I thought you wanted Huck to stop working at the furnace."

"But . . . but . . . " Suddenly, nothing made sense. She didn't want Huck at the furnace, and she didn't want him fired.

Angus continued. "Huck's no good to me the way he is, getting into fights every day and delaying production. He's

191

got to get along, or get out." He headed toward the door. "I'm taking Flora, your mother, and Stubby for a walk. Want to come?"

"No, thank you," she replied absently, her mind in a whirl over Huck's situation at the furnace.

The next morning when Lavinia gazed at herself in the mirror, she realized that the face that stared back at her was anything but pretty. Dark circles had formed under her eyes and a sick pallor had replaced the color in her cheeks. She looked like she hadn't slept all night, and she hadn't. Her father's threat to let Huck go, Flora's scolding over her treatment of him, Toby's concern over his health, and most of all, her own misery since the evening of her birthday had worked on her mind.

In the dark of night, she had made her way to the parlor, lit a lamp, and searched scripture for an answer to her dilemma. She had found it in Ecclesiastes. *To every thing there is a season, and a time to every purpose under heaven.* This was a time to love—*her* time to love *Huck.*

She could not stay away from him any longer. She must go to him and she must do it now. The dinner whistle would blow soon and she would meet up with him outside the casting house. The thought of an encounter with him put her nerves on edge and set her heart aflutter. She silently rehearsed the words she planned to say and wondered whether he would even hear her out.

No matter, she must at least try. She couldn't allow herself to become the reason for Huck's failure at the furnace. *Dear Lord, help me to make things right with Huck.*

She brushed her hair vigorously, tied her favorite scarf around her neck and pinned it in place with the pewter brooch her grandmother had given her. On her way out of the house, she stopped by the kitchen where her mother and grandmother were preparing the midday meal.

"Mama, Grandma, I'm going for a walk," she quietly informed them.

They gazed at her in surprise, her mother saying, "Good for you, dear! I'm glad you're finally getting out again!"

Her grandmother said, "Maybe a little exercise will give you an appetite for the chicken we're stewing for dinner."

"Maybe," Lavinia replied, knowing that all would depend on her encounter with Huck.

Stepping outside, she realized that the day had grown hot, hazy, and humid. The stench of furnace smoke hung in the still air and the birds greeted her with a scolding rather than a pretty song. She pushed those thoughts aside. Swift footsteps carried her over the crushed limestone road to town. Within a few short minutes she stood outside the casting house. Her pulse racing, she paced back and forth. A tug had cast off from the dock and was heading out of the harbor. A barge remained dockside, unloading iron ore. The dinner whistle blew. Men streamed out of the building—Mr. Reilly and Mr. Roempke, Paddy O'Connell and the huge fellow, Arthur Walters. At last, her father emerged, a huge smile appearing when he saw her.

"Lavinia! What a pleasant surprise! I didn't expect company on my walk home for dinner."

"I was looking for Huck. You didn't let him go already, did you?"

Angus shook his head. "He came to me this morning and asked for three days off. He'll be back Monday afternoon. He's on that boat bound for Escanaba." He pointed to the tug leaving the harbor.

Lavinia's heart sank, her worries multiplied. "Why is he going to Escanaba?"

Angus shrugged. "I didn't ask him. I only said that if he gets into any more fights when he comes back, he'll be leaving this place for good." Putting his arm about her waist, he directed her toward home. "I'm hungry. Let's go eat."

Lavinia stood near the dock, watching the tug ply the shimmering surface of the harbor on its approach. She had thought this moment would never come. She had spent her weekend in a conflicted state of mind, wishing time would fly by, yet fearful about what her next encounter with Huck would reveal. Even a return to cooking chores and walks with Stubby hadn't eased her worries. Her stomach was in a knot, her nerves on edge, her outlook dark despite the brilliant sunshine on this late August day.

The rhythmic clank of sledgehammers against iron spilled from the casting house, mimicking the pounding of her heart as moulders cut pigs and sows apart. Others were stacking iron pigs several yards away. Closest to her was Arthur Walters, handling hundred-pound pigs as if they were no heavier than bricks. Near him, Paddy O'Connell and Mr. Reilly were intent on their work.

A shout drew her attention back to the tug.

"There he is! He's the one!"

It was Big Toby. He leaped from the tug to the dock and pointed to Arthur Walters.

A portly fellow, and then Huck emerged beside Toby.

Walters started to run.

The portly fellow raised a pistol and shot into the air. "Halt! In the name of the law!"

Walters kept going. His bulky form gained momentum.

Huck started after him. Big Toby and the portly man followed.

Walters looked back. He didn't seem to know he was on a path toward Lavinia.

She tried to move out of his way. Her feet wouldn't budge!

Walters barreled into her.

Lavinia hit the ground with a thud, her breath gone.

Walters ran off toward the charcoal kilns.

Huck stooped beside Lavinia. "Are you all right?"

She sat up and gasped for air. "I'll be fine . . . get that man!"

Huck took off after Walters again.

Big Toby closed in. He leaped on Walters' back. The big fellow shrugged him off and kept going.

The portly fellow gave up the chase, out of breath.

Huck pursued, Toby close behind. Mr. Reilly and Paddy O'Connell followed.

Lavinia got to her feet in time to see Huck tackle Walters by one leg.

He stumbled and kicked.

Huck held fast.

Toby, Paddy, and Mr. Reilly fell on Walters, knocking him to the ground.

Men poured out of the furnace, Lavinia's father included, surrounding Walters. The portly man made his way to the center of the crowd. Lavinia hurried toward them, arriving in time to hear the words, "Arthur Walters, you're under arrest for manslaughter in Marquette County!" Pressing closer, she watched as the portly man, evidently the Marquette County Sheriff, bound Walters' hands behind his back, then escorted him toward the tug with Toby's help.

When they had boarded the boat, she heard her father say, "Men, it's time to get back to work. We've got pigs to stack, and one less man to do the job."

The men disbursed, pausing to congratulate Huck for stopping Walters. Paddy O'Connell and Mr. Reilly returned to their posts, stacking pigs beside the dock. Within moments, only Huck and Lavinia remained of the crowd that had gathered. He stood a few yards away, gazing at her.

Tentatively, she stepped toward him, her heart thumping, her mind in a whirl. He moved forward, and she could see now that he had a nasty abrasion on his cheek from his struggle with Walters.

She reached up, stopping short of contact. "Huck, you're hurt!"

He took her hand in his. "I'll be fine, and you? If that Walters fellow—"

"I'm all right . . . except . . . oh, Huck, there's so much I want to say to you!"

He squeezed her hand. "And I to you, but not here, not now."

"Will you come for supper?" she asked.

He nodded and released her, stepping away. "I'll see you at supper!"

She watched him until he had disappeared inside the casting house, then she turned toward home, clouds beneath her feet and a prayer of supplication on her lips.

Chapter

17

At home, Lavinia wasted no time informing her mother and grandmother of the excitement at the furnace and of the guest who would be coming to supper. Then she set about mixing up a batch of taffy tarts. While they were baking, she tried to help her mother and grandmother in their preparation of chicken salad. But her mind was so filled with anticipation of the evening to come that she couldn't concentrate hard enough to measure out the ingredients properly.

In exasperation, her mother finally said to her, "Lavinia, if you persist in helping us, we'll end up serving Huck the worst chicken salad sandwich he's ever tasted. Why don't you take Stubby for a walk? Your grandmother and I will see to it that your taffy tarts come out of the oven when they're done."

Lavinia sighed. "If you insist, Mama. But don't you dare let those taffy tarts burn!"

Her mother pinned a sharp look on her. "Have I ever once burned a batch of taffy tarts?"

Lavinia thought a moment. "No, but—"

"Now go on! Enjoy your walk."

She did as her mother requested, taking Stubby up the trail to the bluff and pausing at the lookout where she and Huck had sat on previous occasions. The harbor seemed more picturesque than ever today, the town more idyllic. Or

197

was it just her state of mind? She headed for home, her anticipation building for Huck's arrival.

The wonderful aroma of freshly baked tarts welcomed her back. Once she had seen that they were indeed done to perfection, she headed upstairs to wash her face and comb her hair. Flora came in from her afternoon at the O'Connells', bursting with excitement.

"Mama says Huck's coming for supper, and that you baked taffy tarts. Does that mean you're friends again?"

Lavinia turned to her, taking Flora's hands in her own. "I hope so, Flora, I surely hope so."

"I'm going to pray for you right now." She bowed her head and squeezed her eyes shut.

Lavinia did the same.

"Dear Lord, make my sister and Huck friends again, and make their friendship last a lifetime so they won't ever be as out of sorts as they've been these last two weeks. Thank you, God! Amen."

"Amen!" Lavinia confirmed. "And God, forgive me for all the times I locked Flora out of the room when I shouldn't have." Looking Flora square in the eyes, she said, "I'm sorry, Flora. Will *you* forgive me?"

She smiled. "I already have!"

The furnace whistle blew and Lavinia gasped. "I didn't realize it was so late! The table isn't even set! Will you please help me?"

"Sure!" Flora replied, braids flying as she turned and headed down the stairs.

They had laid out the napkins and silver and were setting water glasses in place when the front door opened. Lavinia hurried to the hall to greet Huck, only to discover that her father had come home alone.

Her heart stopped. "Isn't Huck coming? He said he'd

198

be here for supper."

Angus smiled. "Don't fret. He asked me to tell you he'd be here in a few minutes, as soon as he'd cleaned up and changed."

Lavinia let out a sigh of relief.

Her father sniffed the air. "Is that taffy tarts I smell?"

Before Lavinia could reply, Flora said, "Yes! And Livvy and Huck are going to be friends for as long as they live. I prayed about it and God will make it so!"

Angus chuckled. "I'm glad to hear it, Flora! Now, I'd better go out back and wash up."

Lavinia returned to the dining room to make certain everything was in place, then wandered into the parlor to wait for Huck to arrive. The hope chest she had received for her birthday still stood in the center of the room. She traced her finger over the heart on the lid, praying silently. *Oh, Lord, make of our hearts one heart, and chisel on them a love for one another that will never wear thin.* Beneath the lid were the pillowcases and hot pad embroidered with trilliums that brought to mind the enchantment of the forest in spring. She amended her prayer. *And Lord, let the enchantment of springtime surround us tonight, and bind us with Your love.*

The sound of the doorknocker set her in motion. When she opened the door and saw Huck standing there, tweed cap in hand, she couldn't help remembering the very first time he had come to supper, and how she had slammed the door in his face. The thought of it nearly made her laugh. "Come in, Huck!"

Her brilliant smile and cheerful greeting set Huck's mind at ease. He hung his hat on the hall tree, then simply gazed at her, finding her shiny brown hair, delightful blue dress, and fetching figure more attractive than ever.

Lavinia returned his gaze, reminded of how handsome were his thick, red hair, sparkling blue eyes, and the strong lines of his cheek and jaw.

From behind her came her mother's voice. "Supper is ready. Come to the table, please."

Huck offered his arm and escorted Lavinia to her place, holding the chair before taking the seat beside her.

When the chicken salad sandwiches, potato salad, deviled eggs, and relish tray had been passed, Angus said, "Huck, would you please ask the blessing?"

"I'd be honored," he replied, reaching for Lavinia's hand and bowing his head. "May the furnace burn hot and the iron flow. May the sun shine warm and a gentle breeze blow. May the sandwiches and fixings be tasty today, and the love we find here last forever, we pray. Amen."

"Amen," Lavinia added, squeezing Huck's hand before releasing it to pick up her sandwich.

When Angus had taken his first bite and offered compliments to the cooks, he turned to Huck. "I suppose you weren't expecting so much excitement when you set out from Escanaba today."

"No, sir, I wasn't," Huck replied, "at least, not until I met up with Big Toby and the sheriff on the tug."

Grandma said, "I've been wondering for the longest time if Big Toby went back to his Aunt Edna's when he left here."

"That, he did," Huck confirmed, "and told the sheriff the story about Walters and that he could find him here at Fayette. It seems the sheriff ignored Big Toby's story until another fellow came forward, claiming he also saw Walters hit the man who died at Marquette. The two witnesses were enough to convince the sheriff to come down here and make the arrest."

Angus said, "Superintendent Harris received an inquiry from the sheriff days ago and confirmed that Walters was still here. He and I were the only two at the furnace to know. We didn't want Walters getting suspicious and taking off before the sheriff could get down here to arrest him."

Mary said, "I'm glad Walters is gone. I was afraid someone else might get hurt the way Big Billy did."

Grandma nodded. "It's good we can put that worry to rest."

Angus said, "That, it is. Now, enough about Walters. I'd like to hear more from Huck about his trip to Escanaba. You never did tell me why you were going."

Huck hesitated. "I'm not exactly at liberty to say, sir, at least not yet, but soon, I promise." He took another bite of his sandwich, searching for a new topic of conversation while he chewed, and thankful when Angus began to tell of the number of pigs produced during the last few days and other news concerning the furnace.

When the sandwiches and fixings were gone, Mary said, "If everyone is ready, I'll bring out dessert."

Flora spoke up. "Huck, did you know Livvy baked taffy tarts for dessert?"

He shook his head.

"Well, she did! And you and Livvy are going to be friends forever. At least, that's what I prayed for, and I know God will make it come true!" Flora claimed jubilantly.

Lavinia's cheeks burned. "Hush, Flora. You say too much." She rose and began helping her mother clear plates.

Grandma joined them, commenting, "You know what I always say. Only time will tell."

Huck remembered hearing that phrase when he and Lavinia were hunting mushrooms in the forest and he asked

her if a pig iron man from Wisconsin would do. He silently prayed that this evening would go favorably for him.

The taffy tart that Lavinia placed in front of him,
mounded with a generous dollop of whipped cream, seemed
to confirm his prayer. The flaky crust and overly sweet
taffy filling melted in his mouth and slid down quickly with
the help of the rich, creamy topping. After his first bite, he
told Lavinia, "I didn't think it was possible, but this taffy
tart is even better than the last one you made."

She smiled, and bit into her own tart, unable to distin-
guish any difference but thankful for the compliment.

When dessert was gone, Angus said, "I believe it's time
to take Stubby for a walk. Mary, Flora, will you join me?"

Mary said, "I'd love to!"

Flora said, "Me, too, Papa! I'll go get Stubby."

Grandma turned to Lavinia. "Why don't you invite
Huck into the parlor. I'll wash dishes."

"Thank you, Grandma," Lavinia replied, her pulse racing as she reviewed the words she wanted to say to him,
now that they would be alone together.

Huck followed Lavinia into the parlor, praying for wisdom and eloquence in the moments to come. He waited
until Lavinia had sat down on the sofa, then took a place
beside her and cleared his throat, but before he could get out
the first word, Lavinia began to speak.

"Huck, I'm sorry . . . sorry for what I said on the night
of my birthday and sorry for any hurt I caused." Her
thoughts spinning, she rushed on. "I've done plenty of
thinking since then, and I realize now that I could never go
to Canada . . . at least not while you're here and . . . "

Huck waited, his heart full of hope.

Lavinia drew a breath and started again. "I should never
have made you choose between me, and your job at the fur-

nace. Even though I worry that you could get hurt, the truth is, I'd much rather be worried *with* you than *without* you. These last two weeks apart have been the most miserable time of my entire life. I love you, Huck! And I don't want to be without you!"

He took her hands in his and held tight. "And I've been miserable without you, Lavinia. In fact, I was so miserable I took a swing at anybody at the furnace that even looked at me cross-eyed! But that's over."

He paused, a new tenderness in his blue-eyed gaze. "Lavinia, I love you too much to have you worried here at Fayette when you could be happier somewhere else. I've been offered a position as assistant hotel manager at the Tilden House in Escanaba. The job doesn't pay much, but it includes a small apartment, and there's a shed out back where I can build furniture in my spare time." He slid from the sofa to one knee. "I'm asking you again, Lavinia. Will you marry me? We can get married up on the bluff in September, just like you imagined, then move to the Tilden House right after. My uncle will understand about the money."

She beamed. "Yes, I'll marry you! But there's one thing I must ask."

At his worried look, she hurried on. "I would never want to come between you and your debt to your uncle. Will you please keep your position here at the furnace? Then, at the end of the year when you've paid your Uncle Sean in full, we will marry. Nothing could make me happier than to become the wife of a pig iron man from Wisconsin!"

Hearing Lavinia's declaration, Huck pressed his lips to hers, finding them sweeter than taffy tarts.

More *Great Lakes Romances*®
For prices and availability, contact:
Bigwater Publishing
P.O. Box 177
Caledonia, MI 49316

MACKINAC TRILOGY by Donna Winters
Mackinac, First in the series of *Great Lakes Romances*® (Set at Grand Hotel, Mackinac Island, 1895.)
The Captain and the Widow, Second in the series of *Great Lakes Romances*® (Set in South Haven, Michigan, 1897.)
Sweethearts of Sleeping Bear Bay, Third in the series of *Great Lakes Romances*® (Set in the Sleeping Bear Dune region of northern Michigan, 1898.)

LIGHTHOUSE TRILOGY by Donna Winters
Charlotte of South Manitou Island, Fourth in the series of *Great Lakes Romances*® (Set on South Manitou Island, Michigan, 1891-1898.)
Aurora of North Manitou Island, Fifth in the series of *Great Lakes Romances*® (Set on North Manitou Island, Michigan, 1898-1899.)
Bridget of Cat's Head Point, Sixth in the series of *Great Lakes Romances*® (Set in Traverse City and the Leelanau Peninsula of Michigan, 1899-1900.)
A SPIN-OFF by Donna Winters
Rosalie of Grand Traverse Bay, Seventh in the series of *Great Lakes Romances*® (Set in Traverse City, Michigan, and Winston-Salem, North Carolina, 1900.)

Isabelle's Inning, Encore Edition #1 in the series of *Great Lakes Romances*® (Set in the heart of Great Lakes Country,

1903.)

MICHIGAN WILDERNESS ROMANCES
by Donna Winters
Jenny of L'Anse Bay, Special Edition in the series of *Great Lakes Romances*® (Set in the Keweenaw Peninsula of Upper Michigan in 1867.)
Elizabeth of Saginaw Bay, Pioneer Edition in the series of *Great Lakes Romances*® (Set in the Saginaw Valley of Michigan, 1837.)

TWO CHICAGO STORIES—*reprints of old classics*
Sweet Clover—A Romance of the White City by **Clara Louise Burnham**, Centennial Edition in the series of *Great Lakes Romances*® (Set in Chicago at the World's Columbian Exposition of 1893.)
Amelia by **Brand Whitlock**, Encore Edition #2 in the series of *Great Lakes Romances*® (Set in Chicago and Springfield, Illinois, 1903.)

CALEDONIA CHRONICLES by Donna Winters
Unlikely Duet—Caledonia Chronicles—Part 1 in the series of *Great Lakes Romances*® (Set in Caledonia, Michigan, 1905.)
Butterfly Come Home—Caledonia Chronicles—Part 2 in the series of *Great Lakes Romances*® (Set in Caledonia and Calumet, Michigan, 1905-06.)

Bigwater Classics™ **Series**
Great Lakes Christmas Classics, A Collection of Short Stories, Poems, Illustrations, and Humor from Olden Days
Snail-Shell Harbor, a reprinted novel from 1870 about Fayette, Michigan, and the iron smelting days

ABOUT DONNA WINTERS

Donna Winters and friends outside the hotel at Fayette Historic Townsite.

Donna adopted Michigan as her home state in 1971 when she moved from a small town in upstate, New York. She began penning novels in 1982 while working full time for an electronics firm in Grand Rapids.

She resigned from her job in 1984 following a contract offer for her first book. Since then, Thomas Nelson Publishers, Zondervan Publishing House, Guideposts, and Bigwater Publishing have published her novels. Her husband, Fred, a former American History teacher, shares her enthusiasm for history. Together, they visit historical sites, restored villages, museums, and lake ports purchasing books and reference materials for use in Donna's research.

When researching Fayette, she traveled with her husband and two dogs to the State Historic Townsite several times. The photographs, notes, and books she brought home expanded her knowledge of the area's history. But most valuable were the guidance and reference materials contributed by Brenda Laakso, Site Historian at Fayette, who continued to research details of Fayette's history until the book's completion.

Donna has lived all of her life in states bordering on the Great Lakes. Her familiarity and fascination with these remarkable inland waters and her residence in the heart of Great Lakes Country make her the perfect candidate for writing *Great Lakes Romances*®.

READER SURVEY—*Fayette—A Time to Love*

Your opinion counts! Please fill out and mail this form to:
Reader Survey
Bigwater Publishing
P.O. Box 177
Caledonia, MI 49316

Your
Name:_____

Street:_____

City,State,Zip:_____

In return for your completed survey, we will send you a bookmark and the latest issue of our *Great Lakes Romances*® Newsletter. If your name is not currently on our mailing list, we will also include four note papers and envelopes of an historic Great Lakes scene (while supplies last).

1. Please rate the following elements from A (excellent) to E (poor).

_____Heroine   _____Hero   _____Setting   _____Plot

Comments:_____

_____

2. What setting (time and place) would you like to see in a future book?

_____

(Survey questions continue on next page.)

3. Where did you purchase this book? (If you borrowed it from the library, please give the name/location of the library.)

4. What influenced your decision to read this book?

_____Front Cover _____First Page _____Back Cover Copy

_____Author _____Title _____Friends

_____Publicity (Please describe)_____

5. Please indicate your age range:

_____Under 18 _____25-34 _____46-55

_____18-24 _____35-45 _____Over 55

If desired, include additional comments below.